WILDFIRE AT DAWN

A FIREHAWKS SMOKEJUMPER ROMANCE

M. L. BUCHMAN

Buchman Bookworks

SIGN UP FOR M. L. BUCHMAN'S NEWSLETTER TODAY

and receive:
Release News
Free Short Stories
a Free Novel

Do it today. Do it now.
www.mlbuchman.com/newsletter

Other works by M. L. Buchman:

CHAPTER 1

Mount Hood Aviation's lead smokejumper Johnny Akbar Jepps rolled out of his lower bunk careful not to bang his head on the upper. Well, he tried to roll out, but every muscle fought him, making it more a crawl than a roll. He checked the clock on his phone. Late morning.

He'd slept twenty of the last twenty-four hours and his body felt as if he'd spent the entire time in one position. The coarse plank flooring had been worn smooth by thousands of feet hitting exactly this same spot year in and year out for decades. He managed to stand upright... then he felt it, his shoulders and legs screamed.

Oh, right.

The New Tillamook Burn. Just about the nastiest damn blaze he'd fought in a decade of jumping wildfires. Two hundred thousand acres —over three hundred square miles—of rugged Pacific Coast Range forest, poof! The worst forest fire in a decade for the Pacific Northwest, but they'd killed it off without a single fatality or losing a single town. There'd been a few bigger ones, out in the flatter eastern part of Oregon state. But that much area—mostly on terrain too steep to climb even when it wasn't on fire—had been a horror.

Akbar opened the blackout curtain and winced against the

1

summer brightness of blue sky and towering trees that lined the fire-fighter's camp. Tim was gone from the upper bunk, without kicking Akbar on his way out. He must have been as hazed out as Akbar felt.

He did a couple of side stretches and could feel every single minute of the eight straight days on the wildfire to contain the bastard, then the excruciating nine days more to convince it that it was dead enough to hand off to a Type II incident mop-up crew. Not since his beginning days on a hotshot crew had he spent seventeen days on a single fire.

And in all that time nothing more than catnaps in the acrid safety of the "black"—the burned-over section of a fire, black with char and stark with no hint of green foliage. The mop-up crews would be out there for weeks before it was dead past restarting, but at least it was truly done in. That fire wasn't merely contained; they'd killed it bad.

Yesterday morning, after demobilizing, his team of smokies had pitched into their bunks. No wonder he was so damned sore. His stretches worked out the worst of the kinks but he still must be looking like an old man stumbling about.

He looked down at the sheets. Damn it. They'd been fresh before he went to the fire, now he'd have to wash them again. He'd been too exhausted to shower before sleeping and they were all smeared with the dirt and soot that he could still feel caking his skin. Two-Tall Tim, his number two man and as tall as two of Akbar, kinda, wasn't in his bunk. His towel was missing from the hook.

Shower. Shower would be good. He grabbed his own towel and headed down the dark, narrow hall to the far end of the bunk house. Every one of the dozen doors of his smoke teams were still closed, smokies still sacked out. A glance down another corridor and he could see that at least a couple of the Mount Hood Aviation helicopter crews were up, but most still had closed doors with no hint of light from open curtains sliding under them. All of MHA had gone above and beyond on this one.

"Hey, Tim." Sure enough, the tall Eurasian was in one of the shower stalls, propped up against the back wall letting the hot water stream over him.

"Akbar the Great lives," Two-Tall sounded half asleep.

"Mostly. Doghouse?" Akbar stripped down and hit the next stall. The old plywood dividers were flimsy with age and gray with too many showers. The Mount Hood Aviation firefighters' Hoodie One base camp had been a kids' summer camp for decades. Long since defunct, MHA had taken it over and converted the playfields into landing areas for their helicopters, and regraded the main road into a decent airstrip for the spotter and jump planes.

"Doghouse? Hell, yeah. I'm like ten thousand calories short." Two-Tall found some energy in his voice at the idea of a trip into town.

The Doghouse Inn was in the nearest town. Hood River lay about a half hour down the mountain and had exactly what they needed: smokejumper-sized portions and a very high ratio of awesomely fit young women come to windsurf the Columbia Gorge. The Gorge, which formed the Washington and Oregon border, provided a fantastically target-rich environment for a smokejumper too long in the woods.

"You're too tall to be short of anything," Akbar knew he was being a little slow to reply, but he'd only been awake for minutes.

"You're like a hundred thousand calories short of being even a halfway decent size," Tim was obviously recovering faster than he was.

"Just because my parents loved me instead of tying me to a rack every night ain't my problem, buddy."

He scrubbed and soaped and scrubbed some more until he felt mostly clean.

"I'm telling you, Two-Tall. Whoever invented the hot shower, that's the dude we should give the Nobel prize to."

"You say that every time."

"You arguing?"

He heard Tim give a satisfied groan as some muscle finally let go under the steamy hot water. "Not for a second."

Akbar stepped out and walked over to the line of sinks, smearing a hand back and forth to wipe the condensation from the sheet of stainless steel screwed to the wall. His hazy reflection still sported several smears of char.

"You so purdy, Akbar."

"Purdier than you, Two-Tall." He headed back into the shower to get the last of it.

"So not. You're jealous."

Akbar wasn't the least bit jealous. Yes, despite his lean height, Tim was handsome enough to sweep up any ladies he wanted.

But on his own, Akbar did pretty damn well himself. What he didn't have in height, he made up for with a proper smokejumper's muscled build. Mixed with his tan-dark Indian complexion, he did fine.

The real fun, of course, was when the two of them went cruising together. The women never knew what to make of the two of them side by side. The contrast kept them off balance enough to open even more doors.

He smiled as he toweled down. It also didn't hurt that their opening answer to "what do you do" was "I jump out of planes to fight forest fires."

Worked every damn time. God he loved this job.

THE SMALL TOWN of Hood River, a winding half-an-hour down the mountain from the MHA base camp, was hopping. Mid-June, colleges letting out. Students and the younger set of professors high-tailing it to the Gorge. They packed the bars and breweries and sidewalk cafes. Suddenly every other car on the street had a windsurfing board tied on the roof.

The snooty rich folks were up at the historic Timberline Lodge on Mount Hood itself, not far in the other direction from MHA. Down here it was a younger, thrill seeker set and you could feel the energy.

There were other restaurants in town that might have better pickings, but the Doghouse Inn was MHA tradition and it was a good luck charm—no smokie in his right mind messed with that. This was the bar where all of the MHA crew hung out. It didn't look like much from the outside, just a worn old brick building beaten by the Gorge's violent weather. Aged before its time, which had been long ago.

But inside was awesome. A long wooden bar stretched down one side with a half-jillion microbrew taps and a small but well-stocked kitchen at the far end. The dark wood paneling, even on the ceiling, was barely visible beneath thousands of pictures of doghouses sent from patrons all over the world. Miniature dachshunds in ornately decorated shoeboxes, massive Newfoundlands in backyard mansions that could easily house hundreds of their smaller kin, and everything in between. A gigantic Snoopy atop his doghouse in full Red Baron fighting gear dominated the far wall. Rumor said Shulz himself had been here two owners before and drawn it.

Tables were grouped close together, some for standing and drinking, others for sitting and eating.

"Amy, sweetheart!" Two-Tall called out as they entered the bar. The perky redhead came out from behind the bar to receive a hug from Tim. Akbar got one in turn, so he wasn't complaining. Cute as could be and about his height; her hugs were better than taking most women to bed. Of course, Gerald the cook and the bar's co-owner was big enough and strong enough to squish either Tim or Akbar if they got even a tiny step out of line with his wife. Gerald was one amazingly lucky man.

Akbar grabbed a Walking Man stout and turned to assess the crowd. A couple of the air jocks were in. Carly and Steve were at a little table for two in the corner, obviously not interested in anyone's company but each others. Damn, that had happened fast. New guy on the base swept up one of the most beautiful women on the planet. One of these days he'd have to ask Steve how he'd done that. Or maybe not. It looked like they were settling in for the long haul; the big "M" was so not his own first choice.

Carly was also one of the best FBANs in the business. Akbar was a good Fire Behavior Analyst, had to be or he wouldn't have made it to first stick—lead smokie of the whole MHA crew. But Carly was something else again. He'd always found the Flame Witch, as she was often called, daunting and a bit scary besides; she knew the fire better than it did itself. Steve had latched on to one seriously driven lady. More power to him.

The selection of female tourists was especially good today, but no other smokies in yet. They'd be in soon enough…most of them had groaned awake and said they were coming as he and Two-Tall kicked their hallway doors, but not until they'd been on their way out—he and Tim had first pick. Actually some of the smokies were coming, others had told them quite succinctly where they could go—but hey, jumping into fiery hell is what they did for a living anyway, so no big change there.

A couple of the chopper pilots had nailed down a big table right in the middle of the bustling seating area: Jeannie, Mickey, and Vern. Good "field of fire" in the immediate area.

He and Tim headed over, but Akbar managed to snag the chair closest to the really hot lady with down-her-back curling dark-auburn hair at the next table over—set just right to see her profile easily. Hard shot, sitting there with her parents, but damn she was amazing. And if that was her mom, it said the woman would be good looking for a long time to come.

Two-Tall grimaced at him and Akbar offered him a comfortable "beat out your ass" grin. But this one didn't feel like that. Maybe it was the whole parental thing. He sat back and kept his mouth shut.

He made sure that Two-Tall could see his interest. That made Tim honor bound to try and cut Akbar out of the running.

―――――――

LAURA JENSON HAD SPOTTED them coming into the restaurant. Her dad was only moments behind.

"Those two are walking like they just climbed off their first-ever horseback ride."

She had to laugh, they did. So stiff and awkward they barely managed to move upright. They didn't look like first-time wind-surfers, aching from the unexpected workout. They'd also walked in like they thought they were two gifts to god, which was even funnier. She turned away to avoid laughing in their faces. Guys who thought like that rarely appreciated getting a reality check.

A couple minutes later, at a nod from her dad, she did a careful sideways glance. Sure enough, they'd joined in with a group of friends who were seated at the next table behind her. The short one, shorter than she was by four or five inches, sat to one side. He was doing the old stare without staring routine, as if she were so naïve as to not recognize it. His ridiculously tall companion sat around the next turn of the table to her other side.

Then the tall one raised his voice enough to be heard easily over her dad's story about the latest goings-on at the local drone manufacturer. His company was the first one to be certified by the FAA for limited testing on wildfire and search-and-rescue overflights. She wanted to hear about it, but the tall guy had a deep voice that carried as if he were barrel-chested rather than pencil thin.

"Hell of fire, wasn't it? Where do you think we'll be jumping next?"

Smokies. Well, maybe they had some right to arrogance, but it didn't gain any ground with her.

"Please make it a small one," a woman who Laura couldn't see right behind her chimed in. "I wouldn't mind getting to sleep at least a couple times this summer if I'm gonna be flying you guys around."

Laura tried to listen to her dad, but the patter behind her was picking up speed.

Another guy, "Yeah, know what you mean, Jeannie. I caught myself flying along trying to figure out how to fit crows and Stellar jays with little belly tanks to douse the flames. Maybe get a turkey vulture with a Type I heavy load classification."

"At least you weren't knocked down," Jeannie again. Laura liked her voice; she sounded fun. "Damn tree took out my rotor. They got it aloft, but maintenance hasn't signed it off for fire yet. They better have it done before the next call." A woman who knew no fear—or at least knew about getting back up on the horse.

A woman who flew choppers; that was kind of cool actually. Laura had thought about smokejumping, but not very hard. She enjoyed being down in the forest too much. She'd been born and bred to be a guide. And her job at Timberline Lodge let her do a lot of that.

Dad was working on the search-and-rescue testing. Said they could find a human body heat signature, even in deep trees.

"Hey," Laura finally managed to drag her attention wholly back to her parents. "If you guys need somewhere to test them, I'd love to play. As the Lodge's activities director, I'm down rivers, out on lakes, and leading mountain hikes on most days. All with tourists. And you know how much trouble they get into."

Mom laughed, she knew exactly what her daughter meant. Laura had come by the trade right down the matrilineal line. Grandma had been a fishing and hunting tour guide out of Nome, Alaska back when a woman had to go to Alaska to do more than be a teacher or nurse. Mom had done the same until she met a man from the lower forty-eight who promised they could ride horses almost year-round in Oregon. Laura had practically grown up on horseback, leading group rides deep into the Oregon Wilderness first with her mom and, by the time she was in her mid-teens, on her own.

They chatted about the newest drone technology for a while.

The guy with the big, deep voice finally faded away, one less guy to worry about hitting on her. But out of her peripheral vision, she could still see the other guy, the short one with the tan-dark skin, tight curly black hair, and shoulders like Atlas.

He'd teased the tall guy as they sat down and then gone silent. Not quite watching her; the same way she was not quite watching him.

Her dad missed what was going on, but her mom's smile was definitely giving her shit about it.

AKBAR TOLD himself he was being an idiot. He'd caught that the hot brunette was working up at Timberline Lodge leading the tourists on "activities." She'd have the pick of a very affluent crop. Tim and Vern were already double-teaming a group of windsurfers at a table closer to Tim, too far away for him to join in unless he wholly abandoned the brunette. But he wasn't willing to do that yet.

Instead, he flashed five fingers at Jeannie; she flashed back ten. They'd just bet who bought the next round, on how many minutes before Tim and Vern got the two women at the next table to join them, despite the three windsurfer guys they were already sitting with.

They pulled it off in four and he patted Jeannie in sympathy as she went to the busy bar to get a fresh round, though he opted for a lemonade so it wasn't that big a loss. Her calibration for timing the effectiveness of a pick-up line was for: "flying helicopters to fire," not: "jumping down into fire." Of course the way Jeannie looked, she didn't have to say anything to gather whoever she wanted, but she was a choosy gal. And while he admired her long form and the fire-red streak in her shoulder-long dark hair, she'd never rung his bells or vice versa. So they'd become friends instead.

The noise level was pretty high. Outside the sun was bright and the wind fresh. That meant that three blocks away, down on the Columbia River, the wind would be snapping. And it was out of the west, so it would peel sharp, challenging waves off the river's surface because the water flow was in the other direction. With the conditions so ideal, it meant that the visitors had worked up large appetites and poured into every restaurant in town.

Again, he let his attention drift back to the conversation at the next table. Not windsurfer types. Locals. He never messed with locals because they made for tougher challenge on the female uptake and the downdraft afterwards could be awkward as hell. Your average windsurfer had two or three weeks vacation, on rare occasions a whole summer, and then they were safely back to wherever they'd come from.

"Activities Director at the Lodge," she'd said. Well, she sure didn't look like the type to be leading Bingo night. But he could see her walking through the woods. Her snug jeans revealed long, well-muscled legs. Her worn hiking boots said they were well used. Her tight figure boasted that she did a five-K trail run before Joe-tourist even rolled out for breakfast. He could picture the wind blowing that long curling hair back off her shoulders as she ran.

Akbar could get to like that mental picture of her. A lot.

"What?" She'd turned to glare right at him. He'd been staring as his mind wandered, which was always a bad tactic. He could feel Tim smirking at him for getting caught.

"Sorry," he scrambled around for a fix. He turned to her father, "I couldn't help overhearing. You're with the local drone guys?"

The man nodded carefully. The mother was practically laughing at him; okay, he wasn't being subtle at all. The hot brunette rolled her eyes.

"Well, you probably want to be talking to that guy," Akbar pointed across the room, "if you want some real-world data." Carly and Steve got up to leave at that moment. As they threaded by on their way toward the door, Akbar waved them in. "Steve Mercer, this is—"

"George," Steve lit up and reached out to grab the man's hand. "Man did your bird ever save our asses on the Tillamook Burn. We logged almost three hundred flight hours on the drones alone, never mind choppers and air tankers. I've got to get you some of the recordings."

In moments they'd crowded two more chairs around the small table and Amy had delivered fresh ice teas without even being asked. George, Steve, and Carly were rapidly lost in techy esoterica that had Akbar's eyes glazing over—too much flying, not enough fire.

In the shuffle as Steve and Carly joined the table, Akbar managed to shift his allegiance—and the angle of his chair—from the chopper pilot's table to the brunette's. He wanted to send a gloating look toward Tim, but figured the brunette would catch it and boot his ass.

"That was a pretty good save. Go ahead and do it," she whispered to him. "But make your gloat a good one, because one is all you get."

He timed his look at Tim as the brunette pretended brief attention to her BLT sandwich. Tim closed his eyes as if muttering a curse.

"You get him?"

"Got him good. Thanks." Whoever she was, she didn't miss much.

"So, are you going to ask my name, or just gawk at me like a love-struck bull calf?"

"Well," Akbar settled in to enjoy himself as Amy delivered a double-burger with cheese, bacon, and a plate with a double order of onion rings. "I could be easily talked into just gawking if that works for you."

Her mom had a great laugh. So he turned to her.

"Maybe she secretly likes being gawked at. What do you think?"

"I think, young man, that you're right on the narrow edge of receiving a sharp poke in the ribs. So don't stop now. I'm Jane, Jane Jenson."

"Dad is George. Mom is Jane." He turned back to the brunette. "Does that make you, Judy? Little brother Elroy in space school? Let me guess, you don't have a dog, but the cat was named Astro." He'd been ready for it; the nameless woman's sharp poke bounced off his tightened gut muscles.

"She's my only daughter, but you're dead on about what she named the cat." Jane then prompted him, "Ask her middle name."

"Don't!" the brunette warned.

Akbar fought the smile, he really did, but it wasn't working. Jane was funny and obviously enjoyed torturing her daughter. George was on about something that could easily be space age and he, Carly, and Steve were paying no attention to the rest of the table. So Jane and George Jenson and named her daughter *something* Judy, not quite cruel enough to make her the butt of every *The Jetsons* joke on the planet, but not wholly above it either.

The brunette groaned, then stuck her tongue out at her mother. "Laura. My name is Laura."

"Don't feel too bad. I'm Johnny Akbar Jepps, but everyone calls me Akbar the Great."

She narrowed her eyes in disbelief.

"I know. I guess they love me," he indicated the table of Tim and the fliers. "Can't help themselves. The joke is on them though, my middle name means 'Great.' What parent names their kid Johnny the Great Jepps? I mean, was that the best they could do?"

"Akbar the Great?" Laura Judy Jenson was proving that she had a great smile. "So they're calling you 'Great the Great.'"

"Yeah." He hit the tone of chagrin just right, as if he hated it so much but didn't want to disappoint them, and her smile bloomed even further. *Damn!* was all he could think. For that smile, he'd work a hell of a lot harder than he just had. Her cheeks brightened, the right one dimpled as the smile slid slightly sideways. The eyes that he'd thought were simple brown went golden-honey brown. Her head tipped slightly to the dimple side, which sent her beyond charming and right over into breathtaking.

Akbar felt as if he'd jumped out of the plane and tumbled into freefall. He wondered how much this one would hurt when he landed.

———

Two-Tall went off with a lithe little blond more Akbar's size than Tim's; she didn't even come up to his shoulder. Vern and Mickey wandered off to try the Full Sail Brewery down by the water. Laura had left with her parents and Steve and Carly. Akbar shifted his plate to rejoin Jeannie, the first smokies were just starting to drift in and would find them soon enough. A group of prime tourists jumped on the table the Jensons had just vacated, but he ignored them.

Jeannie ate one of his onion rings, then another as he worked on his burger.

"C'mon, Akbar. Don't tell me that Judy *Jetson* got to you." Clearly she'd been listening to the conversation occurring right behind her.

"Jenson," he corrected her.

"Holy shit!"

He looked up at her which he knew was a mistake as soon as he did it.

"Whoa," Jeannie's offered a low whistle. "She did. I thought no one got under your guard."

He ate an onion ring while she sipped her pint of Belgian Red and studied him.

"Washout? No, I can see that didn't happen. Did you get her number?"

He shrugged. He hadn't.

"Did she get yours?"

"Goddamn Spanish Inquisition," Akbar muttered. Jeannie was tenacious, the same way she flew, and wasn't going to let this one go anytime soon so he answered. "I gave it to her."

"Did she leave it on the table?"

He felt some glimmer of hope. No, she hadn't. Laura had taken the paper napkin bearing his phone number.

CHAPTER 2

Akbar and Two-Tall went for a run the next morning. It had dawned bright and clear and the last of the fire-fight stiffness had to be worked out. Tim had been back before ten last night.

The MHA base was surround by miles and miles of trails. The Douglas fir trees climbed up a hundred feet or more. No old growth in the area, but it had been a long time since the timber here had been harvested. To either side the undergrowth was thick with salal and huckleberry. Old trees that had fallen were disappearing under moss and saplings were taking root in their rotting progenitors. The trails were wide enough for two to run abreast with footing far less tricky than when fighting a blaze in the trackless wilderness.

Akbar had been too tired to harass Tim last night, but after a couple miles he was awake and loose enough.

"Washout?" he asked.

"New Tom Cruise movie in town she wanted to see," Tim sounded really disgusted. "I mean the guy's old. What's he got? Maybe I'm losing my touch. You?"

Akbar hadn't received a message from Laura, but he had some hope yet. Though it would be pretty lame to admit that. "Nah. Brush off, but made good company for lunch."

"Zero for two," Tim noted as they jumped over a small stream and started on the last stretch back toward camp. "We be losing our touch, man. Got to get it back."

They were about a kilometer out, only the long climb back up to the top of the ridge when they exchanged glances. Without a word, they started to sprint up the trail. The race was on.

At a half kilometer to go, an eerie siren sounded over the woods. It didn't pulse and then recede; it kept climbing. Akbar glanced at his watch. It was neither Wednesday nor noon. This wasn't the weekly test.

They shifted from a teasing back and forth run to a flat-out sprint.

MHA had been called to a fire.

Two-Tall beat him to the mowed edge of the grass strip runway by a foot, literally—one massive sneaker's worth. It didn't seem particularly fair.

MARK HENDERSON, the Incident Commander Air, was up in his usual position on the first level of the fire tower that also served as the MHA air field's control tower. It was a two-story structure with a glassed-in hut at the top. A wrap-around balcony circled the upper level of the tower. The heavy wooden stairs had a broad landing halfway up and facing the field. It made a natural podium and the teams were gathering around it.

Akbar assessed the crowd when they arrived. They were supposed to have another couple days dark after fighting the Burn, but Mother Nature didn't always cooperate. It was early enough in the day that most of the smokies were already present.

"Hey TJ," he came to a stop behind the man who'd only just stepped out of the lead jump spot and made Akbar his replacement. "You know, with you out, my team's average age dropped by like a hundred years."

TJ slapped his arm in greeting. "Not one of you damn punks over thirty, are you guys even old enough to know a fire when you see one?" Then he hurried up the stairs to check in with the controllers.

Ox was thirty-five and Chas was forty, but that wasn't the point. Of his two dozen smokies, not a one had under five years in the fire. There'd only been two women so far, but Krista was his number three. It was a good team. The chopper and support teams were of all sorts of ages and had a good spread of women, but being a smokie was tough.

The one thing they had in common, other than a hatred of wildfire, was almost everyone wore fire t-shirts—about half of them were from the Burn. The word Tillamook, half on fire and half burned char, angled down across their chests. "I fought the Burn!" in water-blue letters that dripped down and had doused the fire on the middle of "Tillamook." Akbar had considered framing his, it was one of the best shirts he'd seen in a long time.

TJ now stood beside Mark up on the mid-stair platform listening to his portable radio. He'd jumped over to being the ICG—Incident Commander Ground, opening the number one smokie slot for Akbar. He still missed jumping second to the old cuss, but being on the same two-man stick with Tim made up for a lot of that.

People were still pouring into camp; a number of them lived in cabins nearby. A text would have splashed out across all of their phones.

Henderson casually flashed out three fingers then moved his hands as if tightening the straps on a jump harness. Three more minutes before the briefing started and they would need the smokies geared up. He, Tim, and a number of the smokies bolted into the bunkhouse and pulled on their cotton underwear and Nomex jump suit, including leather boots laced over the pants so that the fire had no chance to sneak up a pant leg.

He slapped the various pockets of his jump suit. A line of rope filled the pouch along the outside of his right calf. Med kit to the left. Foil fire shelter on his hip. The chutes and hand equipment would be aboard the jump plane. He tugged his high collar into place that would protect his neck during the jump and pulled his helmet with its wire mesh face mask from the hook. They grabbed their personal gear bags —which were always stocked with water, energy bars, and dried MREs, Meals Ready to Eat—then raced back out to the tower.

Akbar did a quick scan. The entire first load of smokies was already present and geared up even though this was supposed to be a dark day on the schedule. He made sure he got eye contact with each of the dozen men who were all ready to climb aboard MHA's DC-3 and get gone. They were committed and Akbar wanted each man to know that he was proud of them being prepped and that he was damn proud to be jumping with them. Krista was also suited up and about half of her second load of jumpers were suited. He gave her a sharp nod as well. She'd be ready.

"Here we go," Henderson called out and everyone quieted. "We're off to the Siskiyou National Forest."

There was a universal groan that rippled through the crowd, now numbering over forty between jumpers, pilots, and ground teams. MHA boasted two jump planes, four small choppers plus the heavy-duty brand-new Firehawk, and one of the best crews in the business. Mount Hood Aviation had been in the wildfire business for over thirty years and even with all of that collective experience, the Biscuit Fire—named for Biscuit Creek near the start of the half-million acre fire that had ripped the heart out of the Siskiyou Mountains—had been particularly challenging.

It had hit three years before Akbar joined his first crew, and still he'd heard stories about it like it was yesterday.

"TJ tells me," Mark's voice boomed over the crowd and everyone shut up to listen. He softened his voice only a little and still it carried far and easily. "Back in July 2002 there were hundreds of small, light-ning-strike fires down there, all started in a three-day period. But it was a hot and dry season and firefighters were spread thin, so there was insufficient personnel available to fight them properly. That delay was a disaster and the fires joined and roared out of control. It took from July to December before we were able to kill it off. Well, that's not going to happen this time."

"Thank god!" a number of the older crew muttered.

"So," Mark always kept firm control on his briefings. A former Major in the military—the Special Ops kind—he was fair with the teams and ruthless with the fire. An attitude he and Akbar shared. "I know you all could use another couple days off after fighting the Burn, but we need to kick this one in the ass before it gets away from us. We have fifty acres involved and no one on site. A civilian pilot called this one in."

Mark looked around until he tracked down Akbar in the crowd; only took a moment, find the tallest person in the crowd and then find Akbar next to him. They didn't even have to say anything. Akbar nodded his team was good to go and Henderson acknowledged it.

"First jump plane is airborne in ten minutes, unless you can do it in five. Second plane is ten minutes back. This fire includes all choppers. We'll be based out of..."

It wasn't like Henderson to stretch out something, especially during a briefing. But he did.

"...a field only TJ and Chutes are old enough to remember." That got the laugh and lifted the mood. Akbar could feel the residual exhaustion slide further into the past and realized that even though the man was relatively new to smoke and fire, Akbar still had a lot to learn from him.

TJ made a raspberry noise, but then jumped right in. "Folks, we're going to central nowhere. Shut down in 1981, the Siskiyou Smokejumper Base is only ten miles from this blaze. Retardant tanker trucks are already en route. And any rumors about high times there? Forget about it. Nothing but trees and mountains."

"And fire," Akbar called out.

"And fire," Mark repeated. "Saddle up. You now have eight minutes to get the first flight aloft."

The crowd broke up into a well-organized mêlée.

Chutes McGee, one of the original MHA smokies, was now the paracargo master. He kept the plane fully stocked. Parachutes, chainsaws, Pulaski hand axes, any other gear they'd need was stacked down one side of the plane behind heavy cargo nets so that they wouldn't shift in flight.

They were airborne in six minutes.

Akbar worked his way down the plane. They were an hour out, so he took his time. The smokies were sitting sideways on hard, fold-down seats all along one side of the plane, pulling on the chutes then leaning back against the curved hull of the plane trying to appear relaxed. Only the most seasoned guys would be able to sleep—sure enough, four of them were catnapping with arms crossed over their reserve chutes because who knew the next time they'd get to sleep.

He personally checked every person's gear, using it as an excuse to check in with them. They'd all slept, no one was hung over. Chas had taken a bad fall during the Burn, spraining an ankle and a wrist. But the doc had signed off on his jump card, so he was good to go. Akbar redid the assignments so that Chas was paired with Gustav who was called Ox for a reason; his strength would give Chas a slightly easier time of it until he was back to a hundred percent.

After he got back to his seat, he settled in to do what the ones who weren't sleeping were doing. From the plane's grab bag, he'd dug out a second breakfast of protein and high carbs, then began hydrating as much as he could before the jump.

AFTER SHE GOT BACK from her morning trail run and had showered, Laura headed down to the front desk. Bess handed her the day's signup sheet. Six tourists for a trail ride. All had listed themselves as moderate to experienced riders. Downgrade that to "I've ridden a horse before" through "I have a fifty-fifty chance of getting a horse to go where I want, despite the nice berry bush we're passing."

Then she focused on the names. Grayson Clyde Masterson. One of the ones who'd declared himself as experienced.

"I thought he was checking out?" she pointed at the name for Bess.

She shook her graying curls, "No such luck, Laura. He saw you were leading the trail ride and decided to stay at the last minute. Actually said his meetings at the conference went so well, he was taking the week off and thought this would be an ideal place to spend it."

She didn't manage to suppress her groan, "Aren't we full up?"

"Cancellation. Sorry, but I'm not turning down money."

"Neither am I," Laura agreed. Grayson might be an arrogant clod who thought he was god's gift to women, but he tipped very well. So well that it was a little creepy. Didn't matter; no one was buying their way into her bed and she was saving up for a sorrel she'd had her eye on since the spring. The mare would make a fine breeder and Kenny had promised to hold onto her for Laura at least until the fall.

She flipped through the pages, tomorrow's nature walk was full— and yes Mr. Jerk was one of the people—but no one had signed up for the next day's trail ride yet. So she switched it with the next sheet down and handed it back to Bess. Bess looked down at the new order of events then smiled at Laura and winked. An ice and snow class up on one of Mt. Hood's glaciers. If he wanted to sign up for that, fine.

"I'll fix the activity board." Bess tapped at her computer keys for a few moments. The "Join Us For These Fun Activities" slideshow display screen behind the front desk shifted from close-ups of birds and scenic nature trails to dramatic views from above the Mount Hood timberline, some showing a crowd waving to the camera—each clothed in parka, snow pants, and a climbing harness.

Go ahead, Grayson. Sign up for that one. I dare you.

Laura waved her thanks to Bess and headed for the corral to saddle up the horses. Men were such...

No. No, she wouldn't clump them together merely because she was sick of, well, most of them.

Mister Ed, her big tan gelding, trotted up to the fence line to greet her. They'd been riding together for five years now and the gelding was always anxious when they missed a day. A chunk of carrot and a nose rub reassured him that everything was okay.

She remembered Akbar the Great looking horse-stiff as he crawled in from a fire. There's another thing Grayson wouldn't be doing anytime soon, jumping fire. By the look of his hands, he lifted nothing heavier than a martini glass. Akbar's hands she could picture easily: calloused, strong, and looking as if they could hold up the world.

He'd also been funny and included her mom in the conversation. And he hadn't talked about the New Tillamook Burn other than admitting he was MHA's lead smokie, and only after her mom had asked. He hadn't used his main pick-up card on her. Of course, his buddy had already played "we be smokejumpers" for him. Even if they were in the game together, there wasn't any artifice or hidden agenda about it. They were clear as could be about the question they were asking long before they asked it.

Casual sex was not something she did. But it was hard not to be impressed by Akbar being the lead smokejumper. It was a world where first seat meant something. It was also a world she understood. People like Grayson who made their livings in offices and board-rooms never made sense to her. She liked some, even dated a few, but she'd never understood what drove them. Akbar she understood without even thinking about it: smokejumper, proud of it, and enjoying the obvious benefits.

Like everyone else in all of Oregon, and twice over because she made her living out of doors, she'd read every update on the three weeks that the Burn had raged. From her perch on Mount Hood, she'd been able to see the smoke plume day in and day out; could smell it most days. At night, the hills burned so brightly she'd been able to see them a hundred miles away.

He'd been in that; right on the front lines.

"But the thing I really noticed about him," she told Mister Ed. "Despite being obviously famished for good food after the brutal fire-fight, he kept forgetting to eat as we talked. As if talking to me was more important than anything as mundane as mere hunger. Of course you wouldn't know about that."

Mister Ed who had followed her over to the tack shed and was nosing her pockets looking for another treat.

"He was charming about it."

Mister Ed nickered.

"I know. It's been a long time since anyone did that to me."

Whether by intent, or hoping to discover another carrot, the gelding head-butted the back pocket where she'd stuffed her phone.

She glared at the horse.

Mister Ed gave back one of his "I'm so innocent" looks.

"Okay, fine. But don't tell the others." The half dozen other horses were still snoozing down by the water trough. She dug out another chunk of carrot and laughed as Mister Ed's soft muzzle tickled her open palm.

Then she dug out her phone and sent a text.

"ONE MINUTE OUT," the pilot announced. Akbar and Tim moved to the back of the DC-3 to pull open the rear jump door. He'd woken everyone five minutes earlier and they'd all started selecting which gear the plane's paracargo boss should shove out behind them.

Akbar's phone buzzed.

He dug it out of his pocket. Didn't have time for it, but it might be some last minute instruction from Mark. Wouldn't he be on the radio?

He didn't recognize the number.

Tim popped the rear door and swung it inward. The wind's roar grew tenfold. They were high over steeply rolling green forest.

Akbar hit *View* and glanced at the message. *How about a run in the morning? –Space Girl.*

Shit! He didn't even have time to be pleased, never mind answer. He stuffed it back in his pocket and hurried down the aisle. *Space Girl?* No, she was too much of a woman for that. Space Woman sounded like she was an evil creature from outer space in a 1950s movie. He'd think of something...when he wasn't supposed to be thinking about fire. He knelt beside Tim and looked out the open door.

The fire might have been fifty acres when it was called in, but it was thinking hard about how to reach a hundred. The tinder dry forest was catching fire brutally fast. Flames were crawling up the trees; continuous flame height was around fifty feet. Not enough heat for a running crown fire yet, fire jumping along the treetops, but that wasn't far in the future either.

As soon as the choppers arrived, they'd be kept busy knocking the fire back out of the treetops down to the forest floor where Akbar and his team could fight it.

He grabbed the headset by the door that would connect him to the pilot.

"Talk to me, DC." The pilot's initials were the same as the DC-3 aircraft he flew, so no one used his real name. Akbar wasn't even sure he knew the man's real name though they'd flown together for several years.

"Wind's out of the west at ten to fifteen. NOAA says they're not expecting any major change for the next forty-eight hours. Not seeing a good spot to set you down."

Tim pointed at a couple of possibilities. Damn. Both of them would be tight. Real squeakers. The question was would it be better than a tree jump, purposely snagging themselves in the canopy and then lowering to the ground by rope.

The fire was climbing gullies, creating separate flanking heads, so they didn't dare go down into those inviting gaps between the fires—in case the gap was suddenly engulfed. But if they ignored the fire for the moment, and the winds did hold steady as predicted, maybe they could get to the northwest-running ridge in time. A firebreak along the backside, might mean they could stop this fire cold.

"DC take us down over the ridge at two o'clock low." Tim handed him a couple rolls of drift streamer. He tossed the rolls of crepe paper out the plane's door, spaced along the ridgeline as the plane passed several hundred feet above the treetops. Every smokie twisted in their seats to watch the streamers flutter and catch in the air currents stirred up by the fire.

The brightly colored foot-wide strips kicked and swirled in the air currents like a Chinese dragon on hallucinogens, but there was no windsuck toward the approaching fire...yet.

"Not too bad," Tim said. The ridgeline was far enough ahead of the fire that there weren't a lot of nasty downdrafts developing yet, just the normal mountain madness of winds over ridges.

"There, that's our anchor point." Akbar pointed and Tim nodded his agreement. "DC, set us up for three drops over that bluff you overflew."

He turned to brief the crew, "Three drops. Drop one stick first time," that would be he and Tim as jump buddies, taking the risk and then preparing the area. "Then drop two, then three. The landing is small and pretty cluttered with alder saplings in the ten- to fifteen-foot range. Winds standard for a ridgeline, in other words a normal level of messy, out of the west at fifteen, probably twenty-five miles an hour close to the ground. So, Tim and I will punch a hole. Everyone else get in and clear the drop site to make space for the next team to hit it." Then he thought about Henderson and his teambuilding.

"No idea where the second jumper load is gonna drop in. The nearest decent zone is a mile down the hill. Anyone want to take a bet that's where those slugs come in? At least I know my first-load team can hit it close and clean."

There was a cheer as they began pulling on their helmets and started double-checking each other's gear. It didn't matter that the roster rotated constantly and half of this team could be on the second plane for the next jump. For this moment, they were the best.

Akbar strapped on his own helmet, tugged on gloves and then turned to trade buddy checks with Two-Tall. Once that was done, they both selected smaller chainsaws and clipped them to their cargo lines.

"Race you down," Tim yanked extra hard on Akbar's harness to make sure it was well seated.

"Loser buys first round at the Doghouse," Akbar shook Tim's light frame with an easy jerk back and forth on his chainsaw's tie-off rope.

"Only if I jump first," Tim completed their ritual with a buddy-check-complete thumb's up.

They shared a laugh just as they did before each jump. Akbar was lead smokie. That meant he was first out of the plane and first on the ground.

When DC lit the warning light he braced in the doorway, Tim huddled right behind him. At the green, Akbar jumped and relished the freefall for several seconds. He didn't do a somersault, because he had a chainsaw dangling at his hip. Then he popped the chute and was jerked from a hundred-plus miles an hour to under twenty.

Once he was stable under his chute and checked that Tim was as well, he let the saw hang down on the thirty-foot line. The saws would hit the ground behind his own landing point. The tank of gas in each would be plenty for what they needed until the cargo master could dump more supplies.

The ride down was a little wild. Once, he was sure he was going to eat an eighty-foot Doug fir that was guarding the bluff, twice he was convinced he'd be downslope into the forest before he hit.

But his saw landed on the soft grass and he nailed his spot right between a pair of alders, their thin branches whipping against his helmet's mesh faceplate. He was quick enough to tug the chute closed without it collapsing over the top of some tree. Two-Tall was right beside him.

They jammed their chutes into pack-out bags and fired up their saws. By the time Chas and Ox were coming in, they'd punched a fifty-foot clearing in the center of the alder grove. The other eight dropped in clean and soon the team was ready to get down to some serious work.

Akbar stole a second to peek at his phone. Nope. They were deep in the Siskiyou National Forest. No cell reception on the ground here. No reply to beautiful brunette space lady, at least not until this was done.

He jammed the phone away and did his best not to think about how to apologize for what was sure to be several days of silence.

Right now they had a fire to fight.

GRAYSON CLYDE MASTERSON was being a royal pain in her butt. For one thing, he actually was a skilled rider. It allowed him to constantly maneuver his mount to be closest to hers. For another, he'd appointed himself the assistant ride leader and had pretty much everyone convinced that he and Laura were a charming couple.

At what point do you tell a paying tourist to back off and go to hell? Mom and Grandma had taught her that point came after they paid you. So she slapped on a smile and did her best to stay beside the two newlyweds who were trying hard not to have their first fight during this ride; she was moderately experienced, but he was definitely in the veteran-of-a-single-beach-outing category.

At least the trails on Mount Hood didn't lend themselves to cantering or galloping over grassy fields. The trails here crossed small streams, wandered through forests so silent that sunlight almost made a sound of its own—the horses' heavy hooves dropped almost silent upon the duff of moss and decaying needles.

Laura brought them to a standstill at the edge of a clearing she knew well. Grayson tried to ride forward anyway, but thankfully Exeter knew to pay more attention to Laura than to her rider. The others gathered close beside her. The new groom unintentionally driving his mount between her and Grayson. She snagged Mickey Brown Eye's bridle to stop his forward progress close beside her and the boy let out a huge sigh of relief.

Boy. He was maybe three years younger than she was, yet he was young and eager and happy...and newly married. She was getting tired of not receiving a text from a guy she'd met once in a bar. She was getting tired of shoving aside her feelings... But now was not the time and she shoved them aside once again.

When Grayson went to speak, she shushed him. She pointed to the clearing and settled in to wait. Behind the thin screen of trees, the seven horses sniffed forward, scenting the grass ahead, but she kept them in check.

With a huffed sigh, Exeter and Mickey looked balefully at each other. She wanted to laugh. These two were always making sly comments on her rider assignments for them.

Mister Ed's ears perked forward.

"Watch this," Laura whispered, to make sure everyone was paying attention.

Moments later a Roosevelt elk popped its massive head into the far side of the clearing and looked right at them. The sun caught its long brown muzzle and large floppy ears. For a moment, it almost looked as if its head had been mounted at the forest's edge. Then it broke the tableau by stepping into the clearing to nuzzle the grass, revealing its half-ton of bulk.

Several of the tourists had their cameras out, but she signaled for them to wait.

A long half-minute later, a smaller version of the elk trotted into the clearing, its spindly legs looking far too slender to keep the elk-colt upright. It trotted around its mother.

"Make sure your flashes are off so that you don't spook them," she whispered to the tourists clustered around her and they began snapping photos. She backed up Mister Ed quietly until she could get a decent group shot with her own camera. She kept the elk family lined up in the gap she'd created with her own departure.

"Hey everyone," she called softly. They all turned to look at her, including the mother elk out in the clearing. She snapped the photo.

It was a great shot—the calf had been in mid-prance—definitely her best photo of the season. She'd make sure everyone got one. But she'd have to crop Grayson out before she gave it to Bess for the display board. His knowing leer gave her the creeps. Maybe she'd crop him out of everyone's photos.

Next he'd be knocking on her cabin door. Thankfully her address wasn't listed anywhere.

Well, if he ever did show up, she'd show him a few other things Mom had made sure she'd learned. A wilderness guide had to learn a lot more survival skills than just how to ride a horse.

DC DROPPED two loads of palletized gear before heading over to the Illinois Valley airport. That way he'd be close to hand if they needed anything else dropped in. One pallet landed in the rapidly expanding clearing. The other pallet overshot and hit in the woods, but the chute was in the clearing when it collapsed so they were able to retrieve and pack it without any damage. Then they started unloading and getting organized.

Krista led the second team into the same clearing. Baker snagged himself in a tall larch and had to use a let-down line to get himself out of it. So that gave the first-flight team bragging rights over the second. It didn't last long because Maribel, the second plane's cargo master, nailed both of her pallets of gear into the clearing. Good trick with how damn small the area was.

Once everyone was geared up, he rolled out a map and traced a wavering line in red marker. He checked his watch and wrote "7:45 a.m." at one end of the line. It was going to be a long day. Based on his one look at the fire, it was accurate enough. Then he put a red "X" on the bluff's location.

"This is our anchor point. We'll have Henderson and his air crew narrow the fire as much as they can. I figure we have about fourteen hours, unless things go wrong—"

"And they never go wrong," Tim commented.

"Never," Krista agreed. "Not when Akbar the Great is in charge. Mama Nature wouldn't dare."

He ignored them both and finished his sentence, "—to beat the fire. Krista. Your team starts right here by making this anchor point clean, open it up to a full helispot big enough for the Firehawk in case we need it. Then send your team southeast along the ridge and make a fire trail. I'll be making a line northwest." He drew the two lines along the very top of the ridge's topographic line.

"Deep or long?"

Akbar considered the map for a moment, looked at the shape of the terrain. Right at that moment, Henderson flew by low overhead and waggled the wings of his twin-Beech command plane in greeting. If he was here, the choppers wouldn't be far behind.

"Make the cleared fire trail deep. The choppers will hopefully make it so that we don't have to go too far along the ridgeline to trap this one. It's only a baby, but we are not letting it get away from us. We all clear on that?" He shouted the last as a challenge to the team.

Twenty-three smokies shouted back, "Clear!"

"What do MHA smokies do for a living?"

"We eat fire!"

"Let's do it!" And with a slap of his hands they were off. The first chainsaw was fired off before he even had the map folded and tucked away.

The first of the thin alders to expand the clearing fell before he'd picked up his radio. By the time he'd explained the plan to Henderson, the bluff had been leveled and was in the process of being cleared.

Akbar picked up his own saw. He'd burn through the first tank of gas, leaving the swamping to Tim. Swamping was tough work, dragging all the cut-off branches as far from the approaching fire as possible, but they'd be trading off on the next tank of gas.

He dropped the first tree—the eight-inch diameter, sixty-foot tall larch that had snagged Baker—making sure it fell with the chute on top.

Baker moved in to unsnag the chute he'd left in the upper branches.

Then Akbar began lopping off branches and Tim moved right in behind him with the rhythm of long practice to shift the detritus to the downslope side.

CHAPTER 3

*L*aura had avoided the worst of Grayson's attention by descending to stratagem. She recruited everyone to unsaddle, groom, and feed their mounts. Part of the "country" experience. When they proceeded, as a group, to the Lodge for drinks, she had casually breezed through the "Employees Only" entrance to the kitchen and out the far side to her car.

Once safely off the grounds, she checked her phone. Still no response. Well, what had she expected? Nothing much. So why was she disappointed?

Had she thought that just maybe Akbar had been serious? He had taken the initiative to charm her mother along with herself. It was stupid of her to feel put out. He and his tall friend had made it clear what they wanted right from the start. Akbar, if that even was his real name, had done it with an unexpected grace and style, but it had still been the same old game.

She'd fallen for that trap twice in her life. One of the times she'd actually been foolish enough to think the altar might lie at the far end of the rainbow, only to learn that not just no, but no-how no-way. The only thing lying under Elgin's rainbow had been his wife, who had laughed in Laura's face. She not only knew about it, she did the same herself.

The other had talked a good game, as good as Akbar's—to every girl he passed.

Why had she thought Akbar was any different?

She loosened her hands on the steering wheel after she almost went off the hairpin turn on the way down the mountain and toward her cabin home.

Wouldn't that be the ultimate joke? Careening off a cliff because of someone who didn't even have the decency to call her back.

THE BLOWUP HIT at 4:38 in the afternoon. Akbar had guessed it was coming, had even sent a runner down the line around four o'clock to make sure everyone had their heads still in the game after nine straight hours.

They'd sliced a mile-long clearing fifty feet wide and turned most of it into a bone yard—scraped down to the mineral soil by hand, all of the organics had been cleared out of the fire break. Without the organics, embers would have nothing to ignite.

The fire break ran along the ridge. The choppers had worked a line of retardant to the south until it met with Krista's cut. No fixed-wing tankers available to help; all of those resources were committed down in California and Nevada at the moment. Still, the choppers had done it.

But mid-afternoon temperatures in the Siskiyous had hit over ninety degrees, and the wind was parchingly dry. He'd been able to feel the moisture being dragged out of the trees. And himself.

At 4:30, they'd still had a five- or six-hour window of time to complete their fire break to the north. At 4:45, that had been reduced to half an hour by the blowup. Flames now tore at the sky, reaching a hundred feet into the air and releasing a hungry roar that shook the ground. Shouted orders couldn't even be heard.

The sun was behind the smoke plumes making the sky an evil blood red and turning the day dark. The fire started ripping trees up by their roots and tossing them aside. The updrafts over the fire and the down-drafts over the ridge made it too dangerous for the choppers to get close.

Downdrafts.

He stopped and looked up at the sky.

Tim came to stand beside him.

Akbar pointed.

Tim still didn't see it.

Akbar tried to shout, but his voice was hoarse from smoke and weak from hard work. The air was moving up from the fire; much of the smoke pluming upward and to the east. He traced the downdrafts with his arm to demonstrate. With the intensity of the blowup the low-level smoke was being pulled back in with the air to feed the base of the fire. For the moment, the fire-induced wind was actually blowing downhill, from their position atop the ridge back toward the fire to feed the raging combustion.

"Burn it," he managed to croak out. He grabbed his radio, "MHA Smokies. Burn out the whole line. Backburn now!"

He grabbed a drip torch and sprinted across the fire break they'd spent nine hours cutting and scraping to the very edge of the ridge-line. The monster roared with a hot and hungry breath. Even though it was still far downslope from their position, he could feel its heat radiating toward them, desperate to eat, to consume.

But the fire had made a mistake. And if they were fast, they could turn it into a fatal mistake.

Lighting the wick on his drip torch, he pulled the trigger releasing the fuel. The fuel dribbled out over the burning wick and splattered onto the pine needles and dead branches along the edge of the fire break at the top of the ridge; the edge toward the fire. Even the torch's first tiny flame tips were sucked downslope toward the oncoming blaze, drawn back toward the fire by its own heat-induced weather system.

If they could burn the whole line, sending their own fire burning right into the face of the main fire, there was a chance that the fire break could hold even against the monster coming toward them.

He and Tim headed in opposite directions along the ridgeline, spattering bits of flame as they went. He kept glancing back, saw their own fire building behind him, consuming the dry tinder. Soon, he saw other fires as the rest of the crew got moving.

Back on the radio, he pulled half of Krista's team from the south end to the north. He had to shout to be heard over the massive roar of the approaching flames. It would be a long, hard run of more than a mile over rough terrain, but he needed all the force he could get for the unfinished north end of the line.

"Mark," he called on the ICA's frequency as he ran with the drip torch in one hand and his chainsaw propped over his shoulder, his forearm across the blade, his microphone bobbing in his hand, "hit the north end with everything you can. That's our hole. We can't let it through the gap."

For six more hours they fought the fire back and forth across the ridge. It would spot across the line at a weak point, where the slopes had been too steep to clear well—one of the small choppers would dump a couple hundred gallons and kill it. Steve's drone managed to be everywhere up and down the line, feeding Akbar information almost before he needed it.

The big Firehawk circled back time and again dumping a thousand gallons per load in a shower louder than any cloudburst, a resounding *whomp!* almost loud enough to drown the fire's roar each time. Radio calls flew back and forth, the airwaves a clutter of moves and countermoves.

Twice he sent a runner down the line to make sure everyone was staying hydrated and were solid on their feet.

It was well past sunset—when only Emily in the Firehawk and Jeannie in her little MD500 were authorized for nighttime firefighting—that they finally broke through. They connected the retardant line to the fire break on the north end and trapped the flame.

Around midnight, they declared it contained and Akbar sent half the crew to sleep for three hours. By the time they hit crew turnover,

Krista at least no longer looked cross-eyed with exhaustion. He reported to her that they had kept the fire contained—little chance of it escaping now—and were letting the flames burn out the fuel within the containment boundaries of: the burned-over black, the two heavy lines of retardant to either side, and the firebreak along the ridge. Twenty-four people had made and held a line a mile and a half long.

Now he could sleep for a few hours.

He ate an energy bar and checked his phone.

Still no signal.

He collapsed for three hours and dreamt of fire.

CHAPTER 4

"*The locals still can't* get an engine crew up into this remote corner of the Siskiyou National Forest," Krista told Akbar when she woke him up at six a.m. "They have a dozer cutting in a new road and they should be here before noon. Jeannie and Emily in the Firehawk are both down until noon with the FAA mandated eight-hour break. So, unless you want to walk home, might as well do some work."

"No eight-hour rule for smokies," Two-Tall, splayed out on the hand-scraped soil, groaned as Krista nudged him with the butt of her fire axe. Akbar lay there: still in his full gear, his Pulaski a foot from his hand. He looked up at the sky and saw the soft blue of a northwestern summer sunrise. Not towering flames. Not smoke. Actual blue.

It would be a long slog, but they'd nipped this one before it reached into the next valley. He sat up and looked down the back side of the ridge. Ten thousand acres of now untouched forest lay green below him.

"Worth the pain," he made a point of sounding chipper as he rolled to his feet. Every muscle screamed. He ignored them because otherwise Two-Tall might not look so bad lying there griping about his aching body.

But Akbar couldn't stop the groan as he leaned over to pick up his own fire axe. Tim barely managed a smirk before they both stumbled back toward the fire line behind Krista to do what they could until the mop-up crew made it in.

MR. AWFUL DIDN'T JOIN the nature walk. Whether it was the large crowd, the elderly and grandkid mix he'd spotted as he neared the group, or he really did have phone calls to make, Laura didn't care.

Instead she had a delightful day bird watching, pointing out Sitka columbine and Scotch bluebell, and showing off her favorite little spot to watch deer by a stream. An ATV had arrived ahead of them at the final destination meadow and set out picnic blankets and a large lunch spread. They completed the afternoon with games for all ages in the meadow. The real secret to this loop was, at the end of a very leisurely five-mile walk, they actually had lunch only a few hundred yards from the Lodge; always a happy surprise for the weary.

When she finally got back to her tiny Lodge office tucked beside the ski rental shop, her phone had two messages. The first from a number she sort of recognized simply said, *Fire.*

She'd already hit delete before it registered. That had to be Akbar and it explained why he hadn't returned her call, he'd been on a fire. Suddenly she felt very small and petty. She'd been so angry at him ditching her like that, and instead he'd been jumping a fire.

He could have said a little more than the one word. Not even a *Sorry.* Four lousy characters, five with the period. Maybe that was all he had time for, or the energy.

The second message, about an hour ago read, *Sleep. Run tomorrow?* —FB.

FB? Didn't sound like an apology no matter how she tried to shoe-horn words into it. Was it a *Jetson* reference? She didn't think so. Then she thought of the theme song to the show, "his boy Elroy." *Boy? Fire Boy?* Even if that wasn't right, it was enough to make her laugh.

She sent back *7 a.m. at Lodge.* He'd find the message when he woke up.

Settling into her office chair she did a quick google and found the fire. A small but nasty blaze; small, two hundred acres had burned in a single afternoon and night. The photo, "supplied by MHA recon"— probably one of her dad's drones—showed a towering wall of flame raging against the sky, a chopper in the foreground dwarfed by comparison. Nothing small about that fire. She kept reading. MHA had been on site for just twenty-eight hours and killed it. No wonder she hadn't heard from him. He probably hadn't slept in all that time.

As she finished the article, her phone buzzed with a new message. He sent back, *Glood!* Not awake enough to type accurately, but he'd answered her. She didn't explain her smile when Bess remarked on it. And if Mister Ed noticed before they went out for a ride, he wasn't saying a word either.

"CAN you afford to be so far from base?" was Laura's no nonsense greeting. Her welcoming smile was the only greeting Akbar cared about. Well, that and the way she looked coming down the broad stone steps of the Lodge.

The stone foundation and three stories of wood towered above her. The two main wings stretched off to either side. A central peak climbed several more steep-roofed stories above the entrance, complete with a cupola at the very top. Driving up he'd been able to admire the glacier-capped mass of Mount Hood rising directly behind the Lodge, though now he was close enough that the Lodge masked the peak.

The mass of the building could easily have overshadowed a lesser woman, but Laura looked like a queen descending from the heights. And as she came closer he could really appreciate the rest of the view. At the Doghouse her jeans had suggested great legs, but her running shorts delivered on that promise. And the fluorescent yellow runner's top affirmed the slender waist and athletic chest. When he finally reached her eyes, she was glaring at him—he could tell despite the wrap-around shades—but there didn't appear to be any real heat behind it.

"Damn, Space Ace. You could make this boy want to go AWOL. Mandatory rest day, everyone else is still sacked out." He patted his fanny pack. "Doesn't mean I don't have my radio. Sorry about no response before. Got your message right before I entered a no-cell zone."

"Right before you jumped into it, Fire Boy."

"Yeah." He liked that Laura had figured out the *FB*, but didn't want to play the smokie card on her. It was an odd reaction that he didn't understand. It was a surefire line, "Couldn't call you because I was jumping out of a plane into a fire at the moment." But he didn't want to game Laura.

She waited a long moment, and when he said nothing more, she nodded to herself—whatever that meant. It was a comfortable silence while they stretched out. Akbar had done a full warm-up before the short drive to get here, even done a quarter mile up the airfield and back to work out the soreness from yesterday's fire. He didn't want to look like a total lost cause, but he wasn't going to complain about a chance to watch Laura stretch out. Damn the girl was limber, she was awesome to watch. Which definitely planted some other thoughts in his imagination. Very nice thoughts.

"I have to visit someone before we go," she pulled an apple out of her fanny pack and tossed it lightly in the air.

He shrugged his acceptance.

"A big, very handsome male."

He tried to show he didn't care, but he did. Jealousy wasn't a feeling he was particularly used to and he didn't like the creeping sensation clamping his jaw down. He'd thought her invitation... Then he noticed the teasing edge to her smile and he changed his tack at the last moment. Too late he knew, but he had to try. "Can't wait to meet him."

Her laughed flowed out of her so easily, as if joy were her natural state in the world. That he could get used to; the jealousy shit not so much. Though its tendrils still clawed at him.

She led him around the Lodge and into the woods at an easy trot, still clutching her apple. Laura in motion was even better than Laura standing still. He'd labeled her "hot" when he first saw her. Now he could see that he'd seriously underestimated the situation.

She led him up to a horse corral. Even before she reached the fence, a big tan gelding trotted eagerly over to greet her. The first time he'd ever tested out jealousy, and he'd wasted it on envying a horse. That would teach him.

"And how's my big man today?" she cooed at the horse. She pulled out a knife and began cutting and palming apple slices for the beast. When he was done, she gave him a nose rub and then hugged the horse's big head.

Akbar did find himself being jealous of a horse of all stupid things. They were so close. As she held the horse, the world seemed to go quiet around them. The two of them were absolutely still. The only motion was the gently swishing tails of the other horses in the corral. The only sound, the sharp chatter of a pair of bald eagles riding the thermals high above as they hunted for breakfast.

The smile on Laura's face was so soft and gentle. He could easily imagine how she would look waking up in the morning. Akbar knew he was losing his grip on reality, but didn't particularly want to stop.

"Mister Ed, this is Akbar. Akbar, Mister Ed." She'd saved back the core which she handed to him.

He held it out on his flat palm. The horse snuffled at him suspiciously then took the core with a soft flap of lip. He scrubbed his fingers into the horse's cheek and the animal leaned into it as he chewed.

"He likes you."

"Mister Ed, huh?" he addressed the horse, not her. "So you got caught up in this whole TV thing too, you poor unsuspecting beast. Does he talk?" he turned to Laura. They were suddenly inches apart.

This was the closest he'd been to her, closer even than in side-by-side chairs at the Doghouse Inn. Now he could feel her warmth radiating on the cool morning air. He smelled horse, as he continued to pay some attention to the gelding, but he also smelled a woman like none he ever had before. Like snow and sunshine on the trees. He'd never smelled another woman like her...never expected to again.

"He's pretty vocal," Laura spoke as if wholly unaffected by how close they were; that knocked down his ego a few pegs. All part of the game. "He kept chattering at me in horse the whole time I was trying to decide whether or not I could afford him. He was so chatty, that I bought him even though I couldn't afford to. Called him Mister Ed and the name stuck."

"You my competition, mate?" Akbar addressed the horse and did his best to make it sound funny. To his ear, it sounded right. Inside, it felt a little too serious. When had he ever worried about the competition?

He wished she weren't wearing the shades so that he had some chance to see what she was thinking.

Laura considered Akbar for a long moment. She could hear the slightly false ring of his question, but couldn't pin down what it was. He'd made it sound gruff and macho, as if he was ready to battle a horse for her affections. It was actually one of the nicer compliments she'd ever received. "Hey babe, you're hot," was far more common. It was hard to believe guys actually thought that was charming.

"Mister Ed," she answered him, "is my protector. So don't mess with me or—"

"The horse will pull out his *Jetson's* ray gun and fry my behind. Got it." He turned back to Mister Ed. "You must be one dangerous horse."

She could feel her guard weakening around the man. Actually, she poked around a bit, she didn't feel her guard was up much at all.

"What if..." Akbar trailed out the question and paid Mister Ed a bit more attention. Her horse was loving the strength of Akbar's bare-handed rub down. It made her a little intrigued at what that might feel like. "What if I win your horse over to my side? Then you're in trouble, right?"

Yeah, she was. If she was picturing how it would feel to have this guy's hands on her instead of her horse, she was in deep trouble. Time for a subject change.

"Let's run. I have a group to lead in two hours."

As they set off, Mister Ed nickered at them; he wanted to come along. But which of them was it that he wanted to follow? She wanted to shout traitor over her shoulder.

When they reached the trail and it narrowed too much to run side by side, Akbar waved her ahead. Instead, she dropped back and gave him the lead. She wasn't used to running with anyone else other than her mom, and didn't like the idea of him staring at her from a pace behind. Of course now she was doing the same thing.

He might not have her height or length of leg, but she could see he was a powerful runner. A long, solid stride, very self-assured on the smooth trail. Used to running over untracked terrain among burning trees, this must be a cakewalk for him. But he wasn't just a runner. From his trim waist up, he had a powerful build from hour upon hour of backbreaking labor.

They crossed a fast-rushing stream. He didn't bother making the small detour up to the split-log footbridge, but trotted agilely over the protruding rocks with a quick set of almost dance-like steps and hit the far side in a clean stride.

"What's it like?"

He didn't ask for clarification as he slowed enough that conversation would be easier. "Fighting fire is like nothing else in the world. It has all of the intensity of an avalanche, with more safety and controls than you probably have when you guide tourists on a ride."

Laura couldn't believe that he was translating it into her terms. Nobody was that thoughtful, unless they were making it up. He didn't feel false. Actually, he'd probably learned this trick so long ago that it was automatic: figure out the woman's metaphors and use those to charm her. He was good at it. That it was planned didn't make it any less thoughtful. She let her silence prompt him for more.

"If you get in really close to the main fire, that usually means that things aren't going well. Small stuff we can get in close, but the bull-roarers we try to anticipate rather than attack. It's like a jigsaw puzzle." At a "Y" in the trail, he turned upslope.

She didn't point out that farther on, his choice became a significantly tougher route.

"No two fires are the same. Even one fire can change its behavior from one minute to the next." He eased the pace on the steeper terrain so that he could keep talking, but didn't flag at all as they continued to ascend.

They were at six thousand feet and the thinning air slowed most people down. She'd been up here for the last six months, so she was fully adapted. Apparently his lung capacity was sufficient. Of course, he'd just been fighting a fire at over five thousand feet.

"So, we do our best to be smarter than the fire and—"

"Smarter? Fire's think?"

"In the most evil ways you can imagine. I can't tell you how many times my crew has cut a line, only to have the wind go through three compass shifts so it actually goes around our line and comes at us from the other direction. Fighting a fire on two facing fronts, that's an uncomfortable place to be."

"Then why—" She cut herself off as they broke above the last of the tree line. She'd always enjoyed this view. Climbing out of the trees, the vista was incredible. It was as if Mount Hood simply exploded into being, dropped that very instant from the heavens. The ski slopes and chair lifts were wrapped around one flank of the mountain. It was mid-August, so Palmer was still skiable and the upper lifts were still going to reach there, but the lower slopes had turned to alpine meadow for the short summer season.

They stopped at seven thousand feet, both breathing heavily, to appreciate the view.

"Then why do I jump fire?" He was winded but not breathless.

She nodded, but felt foolish for asking. It was such a natural thing for someone as macho as Akbar the Great.

"So that I can stand where I did yesterday morning. Here, turn around."

Without asking first, he placed his hands on her shoulders and turned her to face south; his hands were an easy and powerful strength where he left them resting light on her shoulders. The shock of the intrusion of her personal space was wholly overwhelmed by how much she enjoyed the feel of that casual strength.

"Look."

Hundreds of square miles of the Mount Hood National Forest stretched before them. Rolling hills cloaked beneath endless rolls of dark conifer. Occasional sharp ridges of rock sliced upward from the green shroud, crying victory as they soared forth. It was one of those perfect summer days and all she could see was the forest that lay for dozens of miles ahead of her.

"Imagine," Akbar's whisper was so close beside her ear that she felt both a chill and a heat. "Imagine that behind us is a couple hundred acres of unsightly black, nose-biting char and hundreds of man-hours of back-breaking mop-up."

His description was a sharp jar to the senses.

"In front of you though, is ten thousand, a hundred thousand acres of pristine forest. My team and I did that. We kept that forest safe and alive, at least until the next fire. There's no feeling like it in the world."

Laura tried to imagine it. Tried to imagine that she had saved this vast area in front of them... "You make me feel small." As if her life was—

"No!" He cut off her thoughts with a tone as sharp as a knife and whirled back to face him, but dropping his grip on her the moment he did so.

She missed it.

"No. You show people *why* it's important. You, your mom, your grandmother that you were telling me about, you show people why it's worth preserving. Every flower or mountain stream or elk you show people attaches them that much more to the land. If it weren't for people like you, they'd probably let it all burn and not even know what they'd lost."

Laura studied his dark eyes. Saw the passion in them, the truth. No dissembler was present now. This was a different man than the one in the Doghouse Inn. No, it was the same man that she'd met, just not the one he did his best to project. Akbar cared about what he did and cared deeply. He even managed to make her feel more important in the process.

Any rational thought went by the wayside, she simply leaned in and kissed him.

His first reaction was neither possessive nor smug; it was surprise. He didn't break the kiss, but did freeze for a long moment, his eyes wide. Only then did he slip his hands onto her waist. Not pulling her in, just holding her as if he needed to steady himself. When he did kiss her back, it was warm, gentle, and lush. The heat grew like a slow fire until she was lost in the whirl of the flames.

He broke the kiss causing her to stagger a half step.

"Damn, Laura Jenson! Is that how they kiss in the space age? I had no idea what I was missing. Sign me up."

It was a line. It was just a silly line. But it was a damn good silly line.

THEY FINISHED the run back at the corral. Laura had shooed Akbar ahead on the descent as well. He'd given her a lot to think about, like maybe she didn't care if it would only be a short fling—not if he'd kiss her like that again. She hadn't wanted him running close behind her, distracting her thoughts.

Sensing something was up, Mister Ed came up to her on the side away from Akbar. The horse made it a clear and total snub. She kissed the big tan gelding on the forehead as Akbar laughed.

"Well, looks like I lost the first round. Care for a rematch, Space Ace?"

"Space Ace?" As nice a request for a second meeting—second date? —as she'd ever received.

"You're out of this world, Laura. And I'm willing to bet you're not even from this millennia. They just don't make women as attractive as you."

There was no question in her mind about wanting a rematch. But he'd be back on call tomorrow, and who knew what that meant. She had to buy herself a moment.

"What do you think?" she asked her horse. Then she reached to scratch the twitchy spot up under his mane.

Mister Ed stretched out his neck and shook his head with a sharp "no" just like he always did when she rubbed that spot.

"Well, there's one thumb's down, Mr. the Great." Akbar tried to pout, but it didn't look very convincing. Then she had an idea as she pictured the day's activity sign-up sheet.

"What? That's an evil grin you've got there."

"Who said today's match was over?" She turned to face Akbar and Mister Ed mirrored her move so they were both staring at him. She couldn't have orchestrated it better if she'd tried. "That was only round one, if you're up for it."

"If you're involved, Space Ace, I'm up for it."

Picturing a firefighter climbing a glacier could be fun. Besides...

"I have to warn you. There will be this big, very handsome male along."

"As handsome as this one?" he nodded toward Mister Ed who continued to eye him suspiciously.

"He certainly thinks so," she allowed the chagrin into her voice.

Akbar flashed her a huge smile, his teeth bright against his skin. "Can't wait to meet him!"

CHAPTER 5

The feeling was not mutual. Grayson Masterson was six-two, square-jawed, and had offered Akbar an overly-powerful handshake when they met. Akbar restrained himself from returning the favor by perhaps crushing a few bones with his fire-fighter-strong grip, and simply returned the same as he received.

He had to remind himself that this was one of Laura's paying guests, and at no small fee. He'd seen the price that Bess wrote off at the front desk when Laura had added him to the list as a personal guest. He'd actually felt a little guilty, but Bess had cut off his protest.

"You'll earn it, young man," she told him without explaining. "Besides, you're the first 'personal guest' Laura has ever signed up even though it's one of her job perks. I look forward to hearing more about you." She offered him a broad wink and turned to other tasks.

Then he'd turned around and looked up into Garyson Masterson's face glaring down at him from on high. The "you'll earn it" part of Bess' statement began to make sense. Grayson had tried sticking close to Laura as she organized everybody, but eight people had signed up for the outing and that kept her moving around.

She slowly got them settled around a large table in one corner of the main hall. People were fetching coffee and tea, he went for hot cocoa himself and settled in to look around.

He'd been up at the Lodge several times. He'd had the pleasure of escorting a few fine women to their rooms, but had never lingered in the grand, central space. The open timber walls soared upward for stories. Heavy beams gave the room a feeling of age-old strength without becoming oppressive. A massive stone fireplace stood like a great pillar. The old WPA guys back in the Depression really knew how to build; this place was gorgeous. He could settle in right here and never move. It was comfortable and airy and cozy all at once.

As the others came to the table, Akbar sized them up. Grayson was gym-fit and arrogant about it, exactly the sort of guy who didn't make it past the first day of firefighter tryouts. No room for attitude on a crew.

Maximilian and Millie were in their sixties but were aging very gracefully; their Austrian accents and good manners would make them pleasant companions for the day.

Jeff and Kris were on their honeymoon. He was teasing her, "if I rode horses for you, you can climb some ice." They were pretty damn cute together; early twenties and looking awfully happy about it.

On Akbar's list marriage had always been in the "someday for sure" category whenever his mom had asked. For these two it had clearly been more of a "can't wait." He didn't wonder too hard what it would take to make him feel that way. Because when he briefly considered it, the whole "marriage someday" concept didn't sound as foreign as it might have even last week. A woman like Laura made it easy for him to imagine that there actually might be a woman out there that he'd actually want to spend a some time with. And that extended into "a lot of time" or even "a lifetime" and he definitely wasn't ready for any of those thoughts.

The other three members of the group were a dad and two teens: Bart, Sammy, and Tiffany. Kids. He didn't have much to do with kids. His own sister, and hence her friends, had been older. He'd managed to snag a full-time slot with MHA his first year out of high school because they were expanding the crews. He'd only thought to take a year off before going to college. Two years in he'd made the jump team and worked his way up for most of a decade. Now, with TJ out, he was the lead. He dealt with the eighteen year olds who tried out for his crew, but this boy and girl were twelve and thirteen.

Laura breezed right up to them, greeted them by name, and soon had them laughing. Tiffany was the outdoorsy one and was all gung-ho. Sammy, not so much. But by the time Laura was done with him, he appeared to have a bit of a crush on her and that would definitely see him up the mountain.

Akbar had a bit of a crush on Ms. Laura Jenson himself and was rather enjoying the sensation.

Once they were all gathered, Laura did the safety lecture thing. Always roped together on the ice. Move slow. Think before you act. All of the basics. He listened with one ear; she didn't miss a single point. Not so Mr. Handsome. He appeared bored with it all, forcing Laura to repeat and emphasize points that everyone else already had gotten.

Akbar sighed. He'd thought this would be fun, helping Laura put an overeager tourist in his place. Now he'd have to actually keep an eye on the guy.

———

LAURA HERDED everyone through the rental shop. The price for the outing included the rental of parka, snow pants, boots, ice axe, helmet, and crampons. It also included transportation up onto the snowfields.

They hiked through the meadow over to the base of the Magic Mile chair lift, most of their gear in lightweight packs and carrying their coats. At the lift she had them shrug into their coats, despite the warm day. The chair was a quad, seating four at a time and it would be much cooler a thousand feet up the mountain. And the Magic Mile was a fast chair generating surprising amounts of wind chill. She sent the Austrians and the newlyweds up in one quad, the dad and his kids next, then she took Akbar and Grayson with her.

Akbar offered her the outside, but she didn't want this to turn into

51

a mano-a-mano thing. The slightest shake of her head and he moved to the outside; if Grayson noticed, he didn't let on. The arm went around behind her along the back of the chair. She had to hide her smile as Akbar apologized for accidentally whacking Grayson's hand when he casually rested his ice axe between them.

She turned to try and mouth an apology for getting him in the middle of this. He cut her off with an easy smile and some stupid question about the skiing conditions at the top of the mountain.

One thing that was unique about Mount Hood was that the top of the Timberline Lodge Ski Area was open year round. The only area in North America that could make the claim, though the last couple of years they'd had to close from mid-September to mid-October. But the summer ski schools and Olympics training were running hot and heavy this August.

Between them, they kept the topic going for the whole ride.

On the upper stretches of a slope called Kipp's Run, they practiced rope work with crampons—mostly how not to step on the rope running toward you from the person ahead of you to your own harness. Stepping on your own rope was an invitation to making an expected face plant as it jerked you unexpectedly by the waist.

The top of Kipp's still had a good thick snowpack, but at lower elevations was completely melted out, so there were no skiers. Their little group owned the upper slopes.

The Austrians and Jeff had enough experience to manage well. And most of Jeff's tips to his wife were correct. The kids were soon having so much fun that shrieks of laughter were echoing through the crystal clear air. To Akbar, this was obviously old hat. His rope work was at least as good as her own. Though the crampons were a new concept, he had the feel of them far sooner than even the experienced hikers. Grayson was, well, being Grayson.

Ice axe arrest training was always fun. They all took turns. The "falling" person lay flat on their back, head aimed down the slope—the hardest recovery position—while someone else held their ankles. At her signal, they were let go. Once they were skidding along with some speed, which only took a moment on this steep terrain, they'd grab the head of the ice axe with one hand, pull the long handle tight across their chest with the other, and lunge over to jam the pick into the snow. This flipped them onto their bellies. The pick in the snow, firmly clamped by their shoulder, caused their feet to swing downhill. Leaning into the ice axe and their now properly downslope-pointing cramponed boots, they were jerked to an abrupt halt.

Akbar did it perfectly every time once she'd demonstrated it. Even Grayson got it right reasonably quickly. The kids couldn't get enough of it until the increased altitude combined with having to climb back up to their starting point each time finally slowed them down.

She moved the group to the head of the main slope, the first real traverse they'd do. She set up two five-man ropes. She anchored one and always picked the most able tourist to anchor the other. Akbar was the obvious choice. The only drawback was that Grayson and the family would make one foursome and the Austrians and newlyweds the other. Grayson had proven that he was the weakest, and she hated strapping him in with kids. No matter how she juggled it, that's the way it came out.

Well, she certainly wasn't going to put Grayson with Akbar, the man was already simmering. Both she and Akbar had been circum-spect, but apparently not careful enough. Could she help it if her smile grew and her body started vibrating every time he got close to her.

So they roped up at the crest of slope, standing in a line along the top. Hers was: Tiffany, dad, Sammy, Grayson, then her. Akbar's was: Austrians, newlyweds, and Akbar. Each person had thirty feet of rope between them connecting from one waist harness to the next.

"Remember," she told everyone. "Keep close enough to the person ahead of you that there is always slack in the rope. That way it makes a big loop downslope from you and you won't step on it."

There were special duties for the person in anchor position and she started rattling them off to Akbar. His nods punctuated her list easily as fast as she could list them off. He already knew the job.

"If someone goes down, it's your job to shout 'Falling!' as loudly as you can and then plant yourself hard, crampons and ice axe. Even if they arrest in the first five feet, you don't release until they're back up and in position." He nodded at that. She could see the pure professional in him. He was taking this far more seriously than even her grandmother which was saying something.

Then she turned and Grayson was glowering down at her. Upset that Akbar had the anchor position? Apparently Grayson had figured out that was a position of strength and importance. Or maybe his brain was addled enough to decide it was a position of especial favor. He turned and went to stomp off.

But instead of departing in high dudgeon, Grayson stomped on his own line. His forward momentum tripped him on the suddenly trapped line and he went down. He landed on his back and in moments was tobogganing down the slope head first and gathering speed fast. His ice axe remained stuck in the snow behind him. He hadn't even been wearing the leash to attach it to his wrist as he'd been instructed several times.

Laura barely had time to squawk out a warning before the lines connecting Grayson to both her and the boy snapped taut and jerked them off their feet. In a moment, the whole line was down. Out of the others, only the girl at the head of the line still had her axe in her hands, though she too was tumbling. Everyone else had been focused on roping up and their axes were now dragging along behind them, dancing about at the far end of the three-foot leashes attached to their wrists.

Laura managed to get her axe in position, roll, and dig in. But the group's momentum was too much. When the line at her waist snapped tight, with the momentum of four people falling, all it did was flip her up and slam her down brutally on her back.

She positioned her axe, repeated the twist and lunge. She saw Tiffany at the far end of the rope make the same effort. But again they were both snatched loose without any help from the other three.

Kipp's had a steep section that normally ended in an easy run out. Now, in mid-summer, it ended in a boulder field.

She was readying herself to try again when something came flashing toward her.

Akbar, down on his belly, arms and legs up as if he was a gull flying down the slope.

"On three!" he shouted at her as he came close.

She got her axe in position.

"One!" he pulled even with her.

"Two!" he was past her, snagged the line, and slammed it into a carabineer clip on his harness.

"Three!" In unison, they rolled, dug in their axe points, were flipped belly down, and then dug in their feet and leaned their shoulders into the ice axe handles.

The rope snapped taught, slammed the harness into her gut.

She let out a yell of rage from somewhere deep inside and managed to hang on.

She and Akbar dragged to a halt and the rope jerked hard again, then they were still.

Laura was almost sick with the pain of where the harness had cut into her. She kept her face down in the snow for a moment.

"You okay?" he was close, so close. And she'd never been so glad to hear anyone's voice.

She managed a nod.

"You got the anchor?"

She pulled her face out of the snow and looked around. His face was bloody from dozens of small ice nicks.

"You gotta be more careful about how you shave."

He raised a hand to his face and then inspected the dots of blood on his palm. Then he smiled at her. She felt the warmth wash away some of the chill of pending disaster.

"At least your pretty face is fine."

"Rest of me feels like shit."

"You got the anchor?" he repeated his question. He'd done exactly as she would have, given her a moment to recover before returning to the urgent question.

She looked around to assess the situation. She had to squint because the sun was blinding on the snow; who knew where her sunglasses had gotten to. Tiffany and her dad had managed to plant their ice axes well enough to keep them and the young boy off the rocks. The boy and the father looked about ready to have a breakdown. Tiffany was getting her brother to plant his ice axe and take some of the load.

"Think I'll offer that girl a job as junior trail guide."

Akbar nodded, still waiting. Still dug in.

Grayson wasn't anywhere to be seen. She became aware of the tension still on the line attached to the harness digging into her gut. There was slack in the boy's rope, so she had all of Grayson's weight, wherever he was. Probably down a crevasse or a melt out hole. They'd fallen much farther down the slope than she'd ever intended to bring the group. She could just see the other four members of the group still perched at the top of the slope exactly where she'd left them.

"I told them to dig in and not move until I came back for them."

"Yes," she focused back on Akbar. A man who seemed to do everything perfectly. "Yes. I confirm I have the anchor."

Akbar gave her an encouraging pat on the shoulder and eased off the rope slowly. The load on her increased, but she could hold it, no longer having to fight the momentum of the racing slide.

"You three hang on there, okay?" Akbar shouted over to the family. "You're doing great! Awesome job, Tiffany. You were right on the ball."

Laura put her face back in the snow. The man had saved them, and was now proving he was great with kids. What couldn't he do?

———

AKBAR SIDLED down the slope working his way along the line but being careful not to touch it. He didn't doubt Laura's ability to hold twice her weight, but he certainly didn't trust the summer snow.

Sure enough, he found Grayson dangling in a crevice. It wasn't actually a glacial crevasse, one of the great openings in the ice that swallowed whole hiking parties never to be seen again. Grayson had broken through the upper crust and plunged down among boulders. He was partially submerged in an icy stream under the snow. He was flailing around languidly, bleeding heavily from the nose and one of his legs didn't look right.

Akbar shouted down to him, and received no reply.

He pulled out his radio. Within moments, the Lodge had a couple ski patrollers headed his way, then he asked for a patch-through to Henderson. Mark picked up in seconds.

"Hey, Akbar. Thought you'd be taking the day off with some pretty lady."

"I am. But her idea of fun is a little out there from my usual. Any of the pilots around?"

"Jeannie's here."

"Good, can you send her to the middle of Kipp's Run at Timberline Lodge Ski Area?"

"Sure. Right away?"

"Soon would be good," he kept his tone as casual as he could, all easy-going and buddy-buddy. "Oh, and would you mind having her bring an evac basket on a long line."

"Airborne in three," was Henderson's snapped out response. He'd never thought about the fun of harassing the ICA, but becoming the lead smokie just two months before hadn't come with a list of all the perks. He'd just found a new one.

Akbar checked upslope. Laura had the kids and the father all under control, keeping them well anchored. Grayson's situation wasn't going to get any worse.

Barely a minute later the first ski patroller arrived. She gathered up the four adults at the top of the slope where Akbar had forbidden them to move before he'd dropped his anchor point on the line and headed downslope.

Two more patrollers arrived right behind the first, coming down to the middle of the slope. They set up a relief on the line to get Laura off-anchor, though she stayed planted as a safety. Then they drove down a couple of snow anchors and tied the family off as well. They copied Laura and stayed carefully planted.

By the time the patrol had rigged another line and were lowering Akbar down to Grayson's position, he could hear the pounding of the approaching chopper. They were less than ten minutes flying time from MHA's air field.

Grayson was conscious now, swearing up a storm and threatening lawsuits that thankfully couldn't be heard beyond the confines of his hole in the snow.

"Hey!" Akbar considered cutting the line and letting him fall down wherever the stream disappeared to back under the snow.

Grayson's invective was heating up. Sick of it, Akbar pulled out his knife and flicked open the long folding blade.

One good look at it mere inches from his face was enough to shut the man up.

"First, let's hope the man out there doesn't sue you for endangering his children through your stupidity, because I sure as hell will stand witness for them."

The guy snorted again, restarting his nose bleed.

"Second, you're going to tip the lady big time for ruining her nice outing."

He went a little cross-eyed trying to focus on the moving tip of Akbar's knife.

"Third, if I ever, ever find out that you've told a single story that makes me wish I'd cut this line and let you fall, I will hunt you down. Or should I cut it now and save myself the trouble?" He shifted the blade toward the taut line keeping Grayson suspended above the rocks and mostly out of the rushing water.

"Uh," Grayson started nodding rapidly then moaned as that set up enough motion to bang his broken leg into the side of a boulder.

Well, the nod was answering the wrong question, but the man had the idea loud and clear now. Akbar tucked the knife away with a quick flick and looked up to make sure no one had been watching his bluff.

Then he got back on the radio and began guiding Jeannie on how to place the basket litter she was lowering into the hole. Once he had Grayson cocooned and strapped in, he snapped himself to Jeannie's long line and let go of the ski patrol's rope.

After a slow and anxious minute jostling to one side then the other of the narrow crevice, they were clear of the hole. He shot a salute of thanks to the ski patrol and waved at Laura.

The Lodge had an ambulance waiting in the parking lot by the time they arrived. Too many cars, so there was no open spot to land the chopper, but they set the basket down and got the jerk transferred. Akbar repacked the basket straps and detached himself.

"You're clear, Jeannie," he called up on the radio. "Thanks. Have Mark send the bill to Grayson Masterson through the Lodge. There will be no problem with him paying it."

"Emergency Search and Rescue, we charge double."

"I'd go for triple, he earned it," he let his droll tone explain how bad that had been. "You're the best."

"Tell the guys that," she was laughing. "Say hello to your girlfriend for me." And she was gone.

Girlfriend? The small crowd that had gathered just as quickly dispersed, leaving Akbar at something of a loss. He found a stone patio at the back of the Lodge that offered a spectacular view of the squared-off top of Mount Hood. He settled down on an Adirondack chair to wait for Laura to get her charges back to their rooms. The sun was warm and the chair comfortable.

He'd never been big on having girlfriends. Women who he spent a week or even a summer with, sure. Not a girlfriend though. But when he'd seen her falling out of control toward the boulders, his gut had wrenched even harder than if she'd been one of his own team in trouble.

He'd kept an eye on her as he yelled at his own ropemates to dig in, dropped his end of the rope, and raced down the slope toward her. She was a woman of action who didn't know how to give up even though she was thrown down harder with each try. It's what he looked for when testing firefighters, but he'd never before found it in a girlfriend.

Two-Tall was gonna laugh his ass off, but Akbar didn't care. An afternoon with Laura—even one as wild as this one—had been worth it.

CHAPTER 6

*L*aura found Akbar asleep in the afternoon sun; he looked as comfortable as a cat. She generally went for the taller guys, and because she'd lived her whole life in central Oregon, they were mostly pretty conservative white guys.

Akbar fit none of that. He was strong, funny, and had saved her behind. And the tourists. She hadn't been prepared for the jerk to be stupid enough to ignore so many of her explicit instructions simultaneously. She'd have to remember that for the future. Remember it was okay to boot a tourist back down the chair lift because they were a safety risk.

If Akbar hadn't been there... She shuddered and pushed the thought aside. He had been. And together, they'd saved the day. Move forward from here.

She sat in a chair facing his, almost every inch of her sore from the multiple attempts to brake the fall. She'd be hurting in the morning. Trail ride. She could ride Mister Ed no matter her condition. Besides, there was one name she could cross off the list. She'd offered today's people a free ride tomorrow if they wanted it.

"Thinking deep thoughts, Space Ace." Akbar's voice sounded slow, thick with his nap.

"Thinking sore thoughts."

"Don't worry, you'll have a nice tip to make up for it."

She laughed at him, "Not likely."

"Let's just say that if he doesn't want to meet me again at the bottom of a dark hole..." His grin looked evil and she decided not to ask.

"I'm done for the day," more like done in. But she wanted to spend some time with Akbar. Just him and nobody else. "Can I interest you in dinner?"

His smile was slow this time, "I hear the Lodge has pretty good food."

"It does," she acknowledged. What kind of alone time did she want with him? Not a hard question. "Or I could cook? I have a cabin about halfway between here and your airfield."

That stopped him. The slow smile went away, but it wasn't replaced by a leer as she'd half expected after meeting him at the Doghouse. Instead his voice was soft. "You sure, Laura? Really sure?"

She nodded, not quite trusting her voice. This wasn't like her. None of this was like her. But she was more sure after seeing his thoughtful reaction.

He looked up at the Lodge for a long moment.

Laura was half afraid that he was going to refuse her. It was too fast. She was being wanton or needy or—

"I wonder," Akbar said slowly, as if testing the idea. Then he aimed that smile at her and she felt herself melt inside. "I wonder if the Lodge does take-out?"

"Don't trust my cooking?" She tried to feel offended, but take-out sounded wonderful.

"Don't want to waste one moment of an evening with you in the kitchen."

She smiled back at him. That too sounded wonderful.

AKBAR FOLLOWED her pickup about twenty minutes along the highway. It was a heavy duty with a mid-bed hitch that he bet matched a big horse trailer. At the moment it had a couple bales of hay which occasionally tossed little bits of dry grass at him in disdain of his own smaller Jeep.

The first ten miles were winding their way off the high spot where Timberline Lodge perched well up Mount Hood's southern flank. She pulled off on a paved narrow two-lane that looked deserted, maybe used by logging trucks. A mile in, she turned up a dirt lane completely overshadowed by trees. Another hundred yards.

There sat the prettiest little log cabin he'd seen in a long time. It was built of well-chinked stout logs with a generous front porch beneath a deep eave. In all but the most slashing of northwest rains you'd be able to sit outside. A metal roof in a whimsical brass color rather than the more expected green topped off the picture. He won his own bet when he spotted the horse trailer parked alongside a tidy, steel-clad pole barn.

They climbed down and met by the steps up to the cabin's front door, but he wasn't ready to go in just yet.

"Mom used to guide from here, but when Dad got the job in town and she broke a hip in a bad fall, they gave it to me. We built the cabin with timber off this land," she waved at the two-acre clearing. Some of it was a garden, but most of it was a horse paddock and the small barn.

Akbar squatted down and scooped up a handful of the dark soil, soft and damp against his palm. Good stuff. He brushed it off on his jeans.

"I winter the horses down here, summers up at the Lodge. We own twenty acres around. I'm buying a brood mare this fall if I can. Have to expand the barn next year."

Akbar was in love. There was a small creek nearby. He didn't see it, but he could hear it. The trees were alive with bird life. The circular clearing was so perfect that it looked as if someone had taken a cookie cutter to the forest then planted the cabin in the middle. The cabin was at the very north end of the clearing, so it would get sun much of the day from having the clearing to the south, despite the tall stands of timber that isolated it from the world.

The trees. He itched to get in here with a saw. Douglas fir always had a lot of dead lower branches that clung on for years, and Laura's trees were no exception. To help protect the place from fire, he would start with clearing the deadwood off the trunks.

"What? Are you just going to stand there?"

"Yes! This place is amazing, Space Ace!" He could see she was pleased, but he wasn't doing it for that reason. It was amazing. This was the kind of place you wanted to take a woman to charm the pants off them, and here he was at her place. Turnabout might be fair play, but he wasn't so sure he was ready for it.

She led him to the front porch, raised a few steps off the ground. He could imagine her sitting here beneath the long eave on rainy afternoons with a good book. She set the take-out containers on the low table in front of a pair of Adirondack chairs just like the Lodge's.

"I stole a couple of their old ones when they were replacing them last season."

"Still look good to me. Shall we try them out?"

"I've got to shower first. Wash this day off me."

Akbar tried to read the situation, suddenly a bit uneasy. Not a single thing today was going by any of his usual patterns and he was adrift without them. Had Laura just extended an invitation? Or did she merely want to take a shower? He didn't know how to read her. With the women he found in town, the messages and intentions were clear. With Laura—

She took his hand and led him inside. Okay, he liked that message. Inside the cabin was as neat as outside. The front half of the interior was a comfortable living room to the left and a really serious kitchen to the right. His mom would like this kitchen, it was totally different from their one in Seattle, but it had a good feel and a serious collection of cool kitchen gadgets.

Afternoon sunlight filtered in and lit the stout plank flooring and throw rugs. Two bedrooms toward the back with a bathroom between.

He slowed her down. He wasn't about to ask if she was sure again; he wasn't a total idiot. Gorgeous brunette drags you into her house, you don't complain. But she was being a little manic, a little too intense—even for him. And he'd been with some pretty wild and wound up ladies.

"Whoa for a second, Space Ace. Just whoa."

Still not speaking, she tugged on his hand again as he came to a stop.

He used that grasp to pull her back toward him. Her eyes were too wide, her breathing too fast. She was going shocky, now, an hour or more after it was all said and done. How tightly wound was her control?

Unsure what to do about it, he slowly pulled her up against him, then wrapped his hands around her back and simply held her.

At first she tried to turn it into something more. His libido was getting majorly upset with his ignoring her actions, but he forced himself to just hold her, nothing more. Hold her and wait.

Sure enough, the shakes set in. He usually didn't hang around for this kind of shit, but to see Laura's strength cracking under the strain was so wrong. Still at a loss, he waited.

She wrapped her arms around his neck and leaned her face down on his shoulder. Her breathing got worse before it got better.

"Oh god. I almost lost them. I came that close. If you hadn't been there—"

"You'd have found a way, Space Ace. You were magnificent."

"But—"

"But nothing. Mr. Hoity Masterson might have gotten a bit more bunged up, nothing less that he deserved, but he only had a few more feet to fall. Tiffany and her dad dug in the same time we did. You'd have managed fine."

After a moment more, she nodded against his shoulder. She didn't let go, but the shakes began to recede.

It took a good and experienced person to assess what had happened, learn the lesson, and acknowledge that. That she did it as fast as any firefighter was pretty damn impressive. And he had to admit, his body was convinced it was a serious turn on. That, and how she melted against him as the shakes went away.

"Now, about that shower..." Because if he didn't get this woman naked soon he was going to whimper or do something else equally lame.

She nodded, but clung on a while longer. He didn't complain then, or later when she led him into the bathroom.

LAURA HAD NEVER BROUGHT anyone here to the cabin; she'd finished building it post-Elgin. She'd certainly never stripped in her bathroom with a man only inches away. Nor ever been so intensely aware of the man in question.

She couldn't stop herself from turning her back as she pulled her shirt off over her head.

At his sharp hiss, she looked over her shoulder at him.

He was looking down at her waist. His touch was light, but it stung where he slid a fingertip over her skin. He turned her slowly around, looking at her belly, not her sports bra. She looked down as well. The line above her hip bones was abraded a bright, road-rash red.

It took her a moment to figure it out. "The harness. Mr. Jerk was heavy."

"Are you hurt anywhere else?"

She flexed her shoulders, which weren't bad, just incredibly sore. And one of her knees had been kind of sticking to her jeans in a pretty uncomfortable fashion.

"Uh," she felt old, weary, and banged up. "I'm a mess." He was going to beg off. She could tell. He was too decent a guy and he'd beg off. Or he was a jerk who didn't want to deal with a damaged woman. Either way, he was about to be gone.

She didn't want him to go. Not after the way it felt when he'd held her. She'd never felt so safe before, not even when they'd been up on the mountain and he'd been clipped in beside her. And definitely not after the way he'd kissed her this morning.

Perhaps reading her mood, he stepped back enough to pull off his own shirt then gave her an up and down look complete with an over-done leer.

"If you look this good when you're a mess, Space Ace, I can't wait to see you when you aren't."

"Stick around, Fire Boy."

"I just might do that, Space Ace."

Then they finished undressing each other.

Laura had seen her fair share of fit men, but Johnny Akbar Jepps really was the Great. His chest and arms were well-muscled, not like a weight-lifter, but like a top athlete. And his legs, no wonder he'd been able to run the way he had. They looked piston strong. He wasn't merely fit, he was practically carved. Muscles shifted in ripples beneath smooth skin. He actually took her breath away.

They didn't make love in the shower. But they learned a lot about each other's bodies. The soap was a good excuse for that. More than once she forgot how to breathe as he did miraculous things with a washcloth. She'd never been with a man who felt so good. And when he kissed her, with the water sluicing down over them, they could have been standing under a hot springs waterfall for how romantic it felt. Not once did he grab and squeeze, or forget and rub his hands too hard over where the harness had abraded her.

Having someone towel her off like he was buffing the final sheen into a marble statue left her skin tingling and alive. She wanted to drag him straight into the bedroom.

Instead, leaving their clothes on the floor, he led her back out onto the porch. She protested at the door, but he dragged her stumbling across the threshold and out into the open air. The late afternoon sunlight slanted warmly onto porch. The to-go containers still sat on the small table.

"I need clothes," she once again tried to go inside, but he closed the front door.

"You don't get to cover one inch of that glorious skin. It's just begging to be admired."

He conducted her to her chair as if he were a maître d'hôtel, and she wasn't buck naked and bruised. Of course your average maître d' probably didn't serve with manners befitting a better than decent restaurant while sporting an impressive arousal. He dished out skewers of organic beef with peppers, mushrooms, and caramelized onions over wild rice onto paper plates.

Succumbing to self consciousness and a need to cover herself, she placed a napkin over her lap and did her best to stomp down on a desire to giggle at the ridiculous situation. But Akbar didn't stare at her breasts, well, not much. Just enough to make her think they might be very pleasing to his eye. Mostly he looked at her face and her nerves settled slowly.

"So," she had to say something. "Tell me about Fire Boy."

"I'd rather know about Judy Jenson."

"Nope. You already got enough of that from my mom." Had she really just mentioned her mom while sitting naked on her front porch?

"No I didn't."

She crossed her arms over her bare breasts, making it clear he wasn't going to get to look at them again until he answered.

He slapped a hand to his chest as if mortally wounded. "Okay, you win."

"That was way too easy," she complained.

"No. Your breasts are that magnificent. I have no power against them."

"Yet we're out here eating instead of curled up in bed together, which was my idea."

Foregoing his fork, Akbar ate a piece of the beef right off his skewer, taking the meat neatly between his teeth and then pulled the skewer out to the side. "I'm a practical guy. I think we need fuel for stamina."

"Are you feeling weak, oh Johnny the Great?"

"Only when I look at you."

"Far too corny," she declared and folded her arms over her breasts again. And once more he slapped his hand to his heart as if slain.

"Okay, I give. I give." He sat back in the chair, holding his plate and crossing his ankle over his knee. He appeared so comfortable in his own skin.

She wanted to ask how he did that. She leaned back against the chair, but the wood felt cool and bumpy against her back. It made her want to shiver even though the sun was warm against her front.

"Little Johnny Jepps always wanted to be an astronaut."

"What went wrong? Afraid of heights?"

He rolled his eyes at her, then offered a knowing wink.

Oh right, he jumped out of airplanes for a living.

"Then he wanted to fly jets. For a brief while he considered being a pioneer in a covered wagon, but he kept getting cast as the Indian." He made pretend feathers behind his head. "Wrong kind of Indian."

She served herself another skewer. A deer wandered into the clearing and stared at her nakedness. She squinched her nose at it and it looked away, but took its time crossing the grassy yard past her fenced garden as if it was window shopping.

"Mahatma Gandhi was ancient history, so not much to aspire to in the world-changing department. Besides, I grew up in Seattle where the oppression has mainly to do with parental curfews and finishing my meals. Mom was pretty big on table manners as well. Dad teaches English at University of Washington and writes odd bits of literary tales that do exactly what odd bits of literary tales are supposed to do, go forth and not sell. Mom always hoped I'd follow in Dad's footsteps."

"A writer?"

"Not that. Dad was five-eleven and married a very nice Indian girl who was five-foot two. I took after her side of the family which is a crime I only forgive her at Christmas and holidays because it cheers her up, poor thing. All her life, stuck with a tall husband, a short son, and a very nice little Indian restaurant of her own right outside the University District."

"You've practiced this line, haven't you?" Laura realized that she was sitting back and rather enjoying herself. The food was good, the deer was amusing as it finished its first lap around the garden fence and found little to pillage except for a few dahlias that had foolishly stuck their heads out through the wire, and the man was as charming as he was handsome.

"Does it show?" He made an elaborate pout at being caught.

"Storytelling father is sure showing."

"Wait until you meet Mom," then he blanched. He looked right at her, then his eyes slid aside; not down, as in to her chest. Aside. "Sorry, that was way too forward. Don't know what I was thinking. But she'd like you. And not just because you're a knockout."

"Not dreaming of some pretty Indian girl for you?" Some part of him, even if it shocked Akbar himself, had imagined taking her home on approval. That was totally absurd on a first date, and they both knew it. But it had been there and she couldn't ignore that compliment either.

"Mom will be happy if I ever settle down. But you two would get along big time. She also loves to laugh."

Laura had never seen herself that way. She lived alone. Saw her parents a couple times a week, and most of her closest friends were horses. Not a lot of laughing opportunity.

Then Akbar rose slowly to his feet and came to stand in front of her. Keeping his eyes on hers as he held out a hand actually sent a shiver rippling over the rest of her skin.

He ended up being the one who led her into the bedroom.

"OH GOD! DON'T STOP!" Laura's moan was driving Akbar wild. His pulse had anchored between his legs; he could feel it pounding there.

But she'd been so awkward and stiff when she lay down on the bed, that he'd rolled her onto her stomach and started a massage. He'd begun at her scalp, scrubbing his fingers through the thick masses of chestnut hair so soft he'd leaned down and rubbed his face in it. Then he worked her neck and shoulders and along her spine. Only copping a feel of the ever-so-soft skin on the sides of her breasts a few times.

She had about the nicest behind he'd ever gotten his hands on. Between the running, the horseback riding, and the hiking, it was quite amazing. He dug into and loosened up the gluts, driving her pelvis down into the mattress as he did so which was eliciting her current moans of pleasure.

He shifted down to her feet and traveled up each of those long legs, feeling each muscle group let go in turn, working the blood back up toward her heart. When he ran his teeth over her insole, she actually cried out. He'd been with women who responded, and others who not so much. But he'd never been with one who lost all semblance of control and didn't seem to care about it.

Laura rolled onto her back and gasped out, "Don't you dare stop."

It had almost killed him to sit outdoors with her not wearing a stitch of clothing. But he'd had to do it. Had to see her out in nature. The naked Amazonian woman with the trees soaring behind her, completely in her element. Every inch of that long, lean frame of hers dappled by the sunlight. She was mesmerizing.

He did as he'd dreamed of doing as she sat so at ease in her chair, that perfectly upright horsewoman posture of hers absolutely slaying him as she asked him about his childhood for crying out loud. That there was enough blood in his brain for him to speak at all was amazing. He'd thought of nothing but starting at the tips of her unpainted toes and discovering every glorious inch of her.

Now fingers stroked, hair brushed on skin to tease, mouth tasted. She opened to him as he progressed upward, digging her fingers into his hair to hold him in place between her legs as she lit like a fire until she was burning so brightly it blinded his senses.

Except for a few times on the fire line, he'd never seen a woman face danger the way she had that morning. Definitely not a civilian. Laura may have been on ice and snow rather than char and flame, but she'd fought for her life and that of those around her and she'd won. He did everything he could think to show her how magnificent she truly was.

She dug protection out of the bedside table and flapped it at him. Unable to stand it any longer, he sheathed himself and drove into her. Her heat scorched. Her fists beat against his chest even as her mouth pulled his down to lie upon her.

The fire that burned in him roared out of control, burned, flared, and was ultimately doused. But still it did not abate. It was merely, finally, at long last quenched—for the moment. With Laura Jenson, the fire of his need for her felt endless.

LAURA CRACKED ONE EYE OPEN. The cabin was lit by only the faintest hint of dawn in the sky. In the Pacific Northwest, summer dawns were a lazy, drawn out affair, casually strolling across the sky, stopping here and there to smell the flowers.

A shadow passed before the window. On this side of the glass. She didn't need to think to remember. Every blazing second of their lovemaking was crystalline clear. As he had mounted her, later she had mounted him. Not just once either. She could feel herself blushing in the dark. They'd done things she'd never done before. Most men did what they wanted, and that's the way it went. With Akbar, even the slightest hint or gentlest pressure had him navigating whole new vistas that were the ones *she'd* wanted explored.

Calling him "The Great" sounded too remote, too foolish.

"Johnny?" It looked as if he was pulling on a shirt.

"I didn't want to wake you."

She felt the breath catch in her throat. Well, what did she expect, bedding the man on their first date together. She'd known what he was when she'd seen him in the restaurant. It had been a long and wild day—and night…and now he was sneaking out. She was torn between saying something sharp and biting or something pitiful like, "Thank you."

When he moved to sit on the edge of the bed beside her, she still couldn't speak. His hip brushed against her arm and she could tell that a shirt was all he'd found of his clothes so far.

"I'm on call today. I have to check on my team, make sure they're okay and that the plane is all set in case there's another fire. I need to be on base by dawn, otherwise no way would I be leaving your bed."

Okay, she was glad she hadn't said the biting thing. Or the pitiful one.

"I'd love a rematch, Space Ace. Because I've certainly never been with a woman like you."

"Been with a lot of women have you?" she managed a tease in the tone.

"Too many. But none like you."

"And how many times have you said that before?"

She could make out the outline of his shrug. "Might have said it a few times. Never meant it before. I seem to this time though."

Laura liked that he didn't hide who he was. Again, that comfort in his own skin thing. They'd definitely need to talk about that some more.

"How long until dawn?" She knew perfectly well.

She could see his head turn to inspect the uncurtained window.

"Long enough," he declared and fell on her.

Laura welcomed him with open arms and held onto him for every second she could.

Two-Tall tried razzing Akbar for not being in his bunk last night. For leaving the morning before without rousting Tim from his rack.

When neither worked, Tim looked at him strangely. "Is Victoria back in town?"

"Not that I know of." They'd had a couple of good nights together before the New Tillamook Burn had set in. He'd jumped into the fire and she'd caught her flight back to a Boston banker's job. Couple of nice texts back and forth, but that was long since done.

"You didn't go back and get my little blond, did you?" Two-Tall's little blond had been taller than Akbar, though not as tall as Laura.

"Nope!" This was getting fun. Clearly Tim had blocked out the woman at the Doghouse that Akbar had declared a "washout." Well, if that was a washout, bring it on.

He kept Tim going for almost an hour. At first it was impressive just how many different women he came up with from Akbar's past. Then it started to get a little depressing. He sounded even more shallow than, well, he was.

Then Jeannie came by and asked if he'd passed on her hello to his new girlfriend. It was enough to trigger some synapse in Tim's brain.

"No! It can't be. The hot brunette?"

"Thanks a lot," he mouthed at Jeannie.

She tugged on the bill of her LA Dodgers hat as if tipping it to say he was welcome, and headed off whistling *Take Me Out to the Ball Game.*

"You tagged a local?"

"She's not a damned tree marked to cut," Akbar snarled at him and headed over to the radio room atop the control tower to get away.

Damn! He had to get his head together. That line was milder than most things he and Tim teased back and forth about the women they bedded. He'd never reacted like that. Of course, the women he'd "tagged" before hadn't been like Laura.

He climbed the tower stairs slowly. By every definition of his life so far, he'd "tagged" Laura. But he hadn't. Not merely "had sex" either. They'd made love. No two ways about it. How had he gotten to a place where that was the exception rather than the rule?

That stopped him cold halfway up the tower stairs.

He wanted to blame it on Two-Tall, but he feared that finger pointed the other way around. Akbar had been the bad influence. Back in high school, he'd pretty much been a loner. The ultimate nerdy geek—he'd taken every AP class and even been in Chess Club for crying out loud. He'd had so many credits, he could have earned a BA in two years, but never got around to it once he'd jumped fire.

He shuddered at that memory of his former self and continued up the stairs. Then he landed the job as a seasonal on an MHA fire-crew when he was hard up for cash and it was the only work he could find. He hadn't thought it beneath him for long. He loved the work. He'd bulked up, filled out with muscle from the hard labor.

Suddenly the girls were paying attention to him. Man, but the lonely outsider had eaten that up, hadn't he? The ultimate ego stroke.

Drop the "wildland firefighter" line and watch 'em fall. A few years later when he added "smokejumper" to that, they'd fallen on their backs ready to go. Johnny Jepps had been lost in a world of willing women.

He gave them the best thanks he could, but he never gave for long.

Akbar the Great fought fire and mowed down the girls to ease something inside. Some lack he couldn't put his finger on. He stopped with his hand on the radio room doorknob. Whatever the lack was, whatever he'd been hunting for, some part of him had found it and really, really liked the way it felt.

He couldn't wait to see Laura again and let whatever that was suddenly make sense once more.

CHAPTER 7

Laura marveled at their routine. A month had gone by and they were borderline domestic. Another aspect of that surprised the living daylights out of her about Johnny. She'd liked using his first name since their very first night together. It somehow fit him better, as if it made him more who he really was rather than Mister "The Great" Smokejumper.

On that second night she'd returned from the Lodge late because of the paperwork around the accident. As Johnny had predicted, Grayson Masterson had inexplicably left a large tip, a very large one— it was amazing how well he knew people. She was already past half way to owning her brood mare.

She'd arrived at her cabin at dusk, debating during the entire drive from the Lodge if she should call him, or if that was too forward. When she arrived, there he'd been, sitting in that same chair. Clothed this time. Quiet. Waiting.

"From an hour before sunset until dawn," he'd said when she'd come to stand in front of him, "they can't call us out because we can't jump at night. I hope it's okay that I'm here."

Laura hadn't said a word. There were none in her. Instead, she'd taken his hand and led him to her bed. Not a single other word had passed between them until the dawn light once again took him from her arms.

Now they had a routine. If he was called to a blaze, he'd send her a text with the name of the fire so that she could follow the news. If it was a long fire, he'd send a simple *Sleep* on his return. That way she knew he was safe, though he always slept off a blaze at the MHA base camp. She'd offered to pick him up so that he wouldn't have to drive but he'd refused, pointing out that half the time they got called to another fire directly from their bunks. It was a hot and dry season and there were more fires than people to fight them.

On her own side, she'd text him news of the day: what outing she was leading, a good joke someone had told, a snapshot of a black squirrel no bigger than her palm that had insisted on sharing her lunch.

The one time she'd gone out on a three-day trail ride and forgotten to tell him, she'd returned to find he'd almost launched a full Search-and-Rescue effort before Bess had talked him down. After that Laura made sure that he knew when she wouldn't make it back to the cabin at night.

She constantly reminded herself not to expect too much, but it was hard to remember when he made it so clear how much he enjoyed being with her.

Laura was slowly adapting to the constant surprise of a willing and attentive lover. It had its up moments and its down ones, which only made the relationship feel all the more real. Though there were fewer of the down moments than any relationship she'd ever had before.

But now she sat in her truck, halfway up her narrow driveway through the woods to her cabin. It was as far as she could get. The afternoon sun shone on vehicles of every shape and size cluttered along her one-lane track. There were a good dozen vehicles, most of them one form or another of pickup, though a rusty clunker Chevy Cavalier and a sparkling red Corvette were in the collection.

What the hell was going on? This was her hideaway from the world. Not her parents, not… Johnny. Johnny Akbar Jepps was about to get his ass kicked but hard. This was not some goddamn party pad. He was welcome in her bed, in her home, but this was too much.

Her immediate progress was blocked by a massive Dodge Ram pickup with rear dualies that looked even more hard-used than her own Ford 150.

She parked and locked her truck. Whoever they were, none of them could leave until she decided to let them out. It had been a long and harrowing morning. She'd led her first group since Grayson Masterson up onto the ice and snow. Everything had gone as perfectly as it had in the fifty jaunts she'd led before, but her nerves were a wreck. She needed a glass of beer and some quiet time on the porch. She did *not* need a god damn smokie convention.

She had hoped that Johnny might be around, maybe he'd be willing to cook because she was tapped out. And no one delivered take-out a half hour drive out of town.

Now she was hoping he was around so that she could kill him, slowly and painfully in front of all his friends.

She stalked up the driveway, kicked his Jeep's tire for good measure when she passed it. Then she registered the sounds which were echoing through *her* forest. Chainsaws, plural. And the biting roar of a wood chipper.

She broke into a run. This was her land. No one was supposed to be logging here, ever. They—

The spectacle at the end of the drive brought her to a stumbling standstill. Twenty feet of chip truck was parked at the head of her driveway. It was painted glossy black with brilliant red-orange flames climbing the sides. It was the Mount Hood Aviation paint job. Behind it, an equally well-maintained and brightly-painted chipper was shooting a steady arc into the back of the truck.

Three people in hardhats and wearing heavy gloves were feeding in dead branches. She turned to the trees to see a half-dozen of them had people up them. Those trees, actually all of the trees for three-quarters of the way around her property no longer had any of their lower dead branches. The people in them were working so fast that the branches appeared to be falling in a continuous cascade.

"Pretty great, huh?"

"Shit!" Laura about jumped out of her skin when Johnny put his hand on her waist from behind. He wore a hardhat, climbing harness around his waist, and had a chainsaw slung over his shoulder as if it was the most normal thing on the planet.

"What the hell, Johnny?" She waved a hand helplessly at the trees and fended off his attempt to kiss her. He was covered in sawdust.

"Your place is a fire trap, Space Ace. Been making me crazy since the first time I came out here. In a fire all that dead wood cooks off," he snapped his gloved fingers. Then he pulled off the glove and tried again with better results. "Massive amounts of fuel just begging for a fire to rip right through it. We had a promised dark day today, so I invited the crew out to do a little fire mitigation in exchange for pizza."

"Did you think about asking first?"

His brow furrowed for a moment, then he shrugged off the idea. "Can't say that I did. Doesn't matter. I wanted you to be safer. This was something I could take care of for you."

She turned back to inspect what was happening. There were six sawyers in the trees. Another six or eight were dragging branches over to the chipper—swampers he'd called them when explaining how a crew fought fire.

This was his specialty. There probably weren't all that many people who knew more about protecting residences from fire than Johnny.

"We okay with this?" he sounded a little worried. Clearly he was starting to rethink his initiative.

She kept her back to him to hide her smile. It was hard not to feel charmed that he'd recruited all of his smokejumper friends on their day off to help protect his girlfriend.

"Space Ace?"

Laura let him suffer a little longer, but could barely keep the smile out of her voice as she let him off the hook. "You said something about pizza?"

Out of the corner of her eye, she could see him pointing upward.

Masked by the sound of the chainsaws, a small black helicopter—with the inevitable red-flame-on-black paint job—was slowing to a stop overhead and then began descending toward the center of the presently unoccupied corral—the only space big enough for a chopper to land.

The man was having pizza delivered by helicopter? She could get very used to this, but didn't want to let it show quite how much he was sweeping her feet out from under her.

"Did you get Hawaiian?" she took the quarter step back to slip her arm around his shoulders despite the dirt and sawdust that coated him. The chopper touched down and began cycling down its engines.

"Got an extra one. Knew it was your favorite."

Laura couldn't help herself. She turned to kiss him. A cheer and a round of applause from around the clearing accompanied the heat of Johnny's hand holding her ever so tightly against him.

Laura felt as if she'd come out of the closet. For a month, Johnny Akbar Jepps had been all hers. Suddenly she was surrounded by his friends and teammates. And every single one had to check out and approve of their boss' choice in women.

The chopper pilot, a woman name Jeannie, sat down next to Laura on the cabin's porch very early on. She didn't say much, just sat there in the chair Johnny usually occupied.

Laura remembered the red streak in her hair from that first meeting at the Doghouse Inn. And when Grayson had gone into the snow, this same helicopter that had delivered the pizza had appeared to save his sorry life. She was obviously a fixture in Johnny's life, and Laura tried to prepare herself for the upcoming catfight. Laura really needed this day to be over soon.

Johnny had drifted off with some of the others, holding court around her picnic table suddenly buried in pizza boxes, and a big cooler of sodas nearby.

At first she was ticked at Johnny for abandoning her. Was he being unthinking? No. Johnny was never unthinking, but he often thought differently than she did. So he was…being a second center of attention so that everyone wasn't crowded about her at once. She wished he'd found a way to call Jeannie aside, but the woman showed no signs of moving off.

As time passed and one group of smokies drifted off only to inevitably be replaced by a few fresh recruits, Laura began to see what Jeannie was doing.

Somehow, by simply sitting beside Laura, she was placing her stamp of approval or at least easing the start of each successive conversation. The crew drifted by in twos and threes, some chatting with Jeannie for a moment as an excuse to not make it look like the tag-team interrogation that it actually was. Everyone wanted to hear from her own lips who she was, what her background was, her political views and…

It took her a while to figure out that mentioning she was a wilderness guide saved her a lot of well-intended nosiness. It also told her that Johnny hadn't been bragging about her all around camp. Despite the mayhem he'd unleashed on her today, he apparently respected some aspects of her privacy.

That simple "wilderness guide" title was a ticket of first-class boarding priority in the smokie world. She'd thought it was just Johnny who felt the way she did about the wilderness. Laura soon figured out that each and every person here loved living and working in the wilderness. Jumping out of a plane to fight a forest-killing inferno up close and personal was a job most of them would pay to be allowed to do.

Johnny had held off the tall guy until nearly the last. He shot her a slightly worried expression as the man sauntered up to greet Jeannie.

So, this one was important to him. Of course, they'd arrived at the bar together; apparently Johnny's wingman both on and off the fire line.

"Two-Tall, that's t-w-o, Tim, that's D-a-v-e," he offered a genuine enough smile to accompany his joke, and a handshake that wholly enveloped her own hand. "Damn! I can't believe you brushed me off for Akbar the Great. He is short, you know."

"I admit I noticed," Laura's throat was dry despite sipping at her soda. Even sitting on the edge of the porch he loomed, his back casually against one of the posts. All he needed was a cowboy hat and a six-gun slung around his fire gear to look totally, well, out of place.

"But he is great," his teasing expression suddenly shifted to a serious one. "Best crew boss I ever walked fire with. Even better than TJ, but don't you dare tell him I said that."

She crossed her heart.

He chatted a bit more without saying much. But she had the impression that she was being more thoroughly examined by him than any of the others.

After he moved off, Laura observed quietly to herself, "Well, he's a deep one."

Jeannie beside her nodded, "Two-Tall is an ogre."

Laura looked over, but figured it out before she had to ask. Like Shrek the ogre comparing himself to an onion, Tim had layers upon layers despite the carefree womanizer he presented to the world.

Like Johnny Akbar Jepps.

Her lover constantly revealed new aspects to himself. His knowledge of fires was his main focus, but he would often lead her off into head-spinning explanations of the science behind combustion or how the historical impact of the burning of Ancient Rome upon literature of all crazy things. It was as if his lack of a college education and his voracious reading habits had combined to create an intensely out of the box thinker.

Soon the smokies began shifting back to finish the trees. In a matter of minutes, they were back in the woods, chainsaws at the roar. Then they fired up the big chipper and the clearing once again reverberated with the clean-up operation.

She felt she should go help, but knew she'd be in their way. They had it down to a science. Johnny and Tim were switching off on successive trees, taking turns cutting and swamping the cut branches. They covered half again the ground of any other team.

"They're something, aren't they?" Jeannie still sat in the chair Johnny usually occupied. She'd been so quiet that Laura had almost forgotten she was there.

"They make it look like a ballet."

Jeannie nodded amiably, "They're the very best in the business. It would help if they didn't know it, but they do. And only Carly can read a fire better than Akbar; she's scary good. Kind of on the level of our lead pilot Emily."

Laura could hear the worshipful tone in Jeannie's voice. She knew from following the articles this last month that MHA's reputation was the gold standard of wildland firefighting. If Johnny was the gold standard of that... The breath whooshed out of her a bit. What in the world had she hooked herself up to?

"You want another piece?" Jeannie clambered to her feet.

Laura nodded.

Jeannie returned with a paper plate bearing a couple slices of Hawaiian without even asking and another plate with a couple combos, but she didn't sit back down after handing Laura's over.

"Been watching you."

Oh great. She'd been right the first time. Jeannie had a thing for Johnny and he'd been too blind to see it. Now she was going to really catch it.

"If Akbar screws this up, I'm gonna kill him. You're great!" Then she flashed an impish smile and headed toward her chopper as she ate her pizza.

Too stunned to respond, Laura could only watch her go.

Well if that didn't beat all.

AFTER THEY FINISHED with the trees, a fire had been started in her brick-lined fire pit. Cold pizza was inhaled and a cooler of beer had been recovered from one of the trucks. Almost no one had more than one, though, in case they were called in the morning.

They'd sat for hours, talking about fires and, perhaps inevitably, women. Krista, a broad-shouldered Nordic blond and apparently Johnny's other main assistant, sat across the fire beside Two-Tall, razzing the men about all of things they didn't understand about women. She was as brash and salty as many of the guys—funny, but a little out there for Laura. She wished Jeannie had stayed; she would have liked to get to know the woman better.

She was walking back in the dark from moving her truck out of the way, when she spotted Tim and Johnny standing close by the cabin's front porch outlined in the light of the open front door. They were an odd couple, but there'd been no denying how perfectly they worked together. On the job, the two men rarely had to speak, but their communication was obviously crystal clear nonetheless.

"Damn, man, I just don't know." Tim's deep voice carried easily across the still night air.

Laura braced herself. She'd been so happy. Despite the unexpected beginning to the evening—and the intense scrutiny—she'd enjoyed herself. Johnny's team was close-knit and would walk through fire for him. She laughed a little at the metaphor. They actually did that one literally, all the time.

But now Tim was about to pass judgment on her. She wanted to cry out in protest to stop him from shattering one of the best things to happen to her in far too long a time. Johnny had come to mean so much to her, but she couldn't speak. Instead she was forced to stand in the darkness and listen to her fate.

"I don't get it," Tim thumped a big hand down on Johnny's shoulder with a blow that would have staggered a lesser man. "How does a little shit like you land such an amazing lady?"

Laura almost strangled on her next breath she was so surprised.

"You do *not* toss this one over, man. You do *not* screw this up or I will personally beat the living shit out of you. We clear?"

"Hey," Johnny protested. "I thought you were *my* friend. You're supposed to be on my side."

"I am, man," Tim shook him back and forth by the shoulder. "That's why I'm warning you. Laura isn't normal fare. She ain't no catch-and-release. She's a keeper. You remember that or you're toast."

She slid into a deeper shadow as Tim passed by, waited until he started up his own truck and was the last to leave. Then she sidled up beside Johnny who appeared very quiet.

"Thank you for tonight. Both the safety," she nodded toward the trees, "and for introducing me to your friends."

He'd nodded, but said little. After he'd showered, he came to bed, curled up against her shoulder, and slipped into sleep. The poor man must be exhausted.

Laura lay flat on her back staring up at the heavy beams of her darkened bedroom. Moonlight spilled in through the window open to the warm night. The scent of fresh cut pine hung thick on the still air. They'd dead-limbed every tree for almost two hundred feet into the woods to all sides of the cabin as well as clearing the forest floor of any windfall that hadn't already turned into more mulch than fuel. Anything thicker than three inches they'd chopped up into woodstove lengths and stacked under the cabin's eave. In an afternoon, she had at least half a winter's worth of wood put up.

She stared at the ceiling and hung onto the man sleeping curled against her shoulder.

Tim had dubbed her "a keeper." Is that what she was? No one else she'd ever been with had thought so. She'd learned her independence early, because that was all she had to hold onto. Men were drawn to her looks, but that was all. She'd found her peace in the deep woods. Alone with Mister Ed or leading a group, it didn't matter. She'd often imagined someone there beside her, but never found him.

One of the best things that had happened to her in a long time. Yes, that had been her own thought. He actually might be the best thing ever to happen, certainly the best male thing. Well, she'd never pictured a smokejumper with an easy laugh, a bravura manner, and such incredible self-confidence. She also hadn't pictured a man that so many people thought so highly of.

She wanted to laugh. Would have if she hadn't been afraid of waking the man lying so soundly asleep on her shoulder. Instead she kissed him gently on the top of his head.

Of all crazy things, she'd gone and fallen in love with a man named Akbar the Great.

———————

AKBAR HEARD the porch deck boards creak as Laura came out the cabin's front door.

"Johnny?" Laura had taken to calling him that almost from the beginning; he hadn't argued and now was coming to like it. Only his mother ever called him that but he hadn't told Laura, because…well, because it was just too weird if he thought about it. His dad always used Akbar or Akbar the Akbar with a bit of a laugh, *Great the Great.* His big sister usually called him Dipwad; the nickname had been mutual in both directions since before he could remember. There was a little worry in Laura's tone.

"Right here, Space Ace."

It was only an hour or so before dawn. Yesterday's heat had continued to hang on through the night, comfortable now without being oppressive. Laura was wrapped in a light blanket which was more than he wore.

"What are you thinking about so intently out here in the dark?" She slid into his lap and rested her cheek on his hair as his arms slid around her incredible form and held her close. The better he got to know her, the more amazing she felt, which was totally backwards. First nights were supposed to be the best and then the long slow burnout as the initial heat wore off.

Their first night of making love had turned out to only be an invitation, an introduction to the wonders of Laura Jenson's physical form. For a month, the heat had kept building, driven and fanned by the woman within.

"I'm thinking about what an incredible body you have."

She made a fake gagging sound, "Besides, if you were thinking that, you'd still be in bed with me."

Well, he'd known she was smart from the first moment he'd spotted her. Paybacks were such hell. Yeah, paybacks like a beautiful woman who welcomes him into her life as if he'd always belonged there.

"I'm thinking..." he nuzzled her neck and cupped her breast through the thin blanket, "...that I was an idiot and should drag you right back to bed."

"Answer the question, Fire Boy, or get that hand off my breast."

He removed his hand, then slid it down between her legs to cup her behind through the cloth, his wrist riding tight against her.

"Okay," her breathing was distinctly heavier. "Maybe I should have phrased that differently."

Akbar tipped his head and kissed her. Kissing Laura Jenson made him feel so alive and powerful it was hard to credit. It was the exact same feeling as waking on that ridgeline to see that they'd defeated the blaze and ten thousand acres of forest lay safe before him. Knowing that somehow, inexplicably, he was a part of something so amazing.

She brushed those slender, strong fingers along his face and then pulled back enough to speak, but her fingers continued to caress his cheek. "What are you avoiding?"

He tried to shrug it off, but stopped halfway through with a sigh, "Damned if I know, Laura."

She pulled his head against her shoulder and rested her cheek once more on his hair. "Describe it for me."

"It feels..." he growled at his own helplessness then forged ahead anyway. "If feels as if I'm watching a fire, but I'm missing something. Some key element. And if I don't find it, it's going to do a slopover across the control line and I'll have a blowup with a whole new world of hurt on my hands."

"And this doesn't have anything to do with Tim threatening to be my champion if you screw this up?"

"You heard that?" He wished she hadn't heard that. It was embarrassing. As if Tim could see the "something" that he couldn't. And he hadn't been the only one. Krista had pulled him aside and threatened him in that gentle way of hers, something about "taking a Pulaski to his nuts." Jeannie, even Jeannie, had sent him a text message saying she liked Laura and, while she was too good for someone like Akbar, Jeannie would still let him be her friend as long as he didn't screw up the relationship.

"Yes, I heard that," Laura's chest hummed against his ear. "I don't think he gets how far that deep voice of his carries."

Akbar sighed. "Yeah, I used to think the same thing. Tim doesn't miss that kind of thing. He must have known you were nearby."

"So, I'm guessing he's not the only one who has thrown you over for me and that's freaking you out."

"No," Akbar ground it out. "That's not what's freaking me out. I don't think." Pissing him off a bit? Yeah. Confusing the daylights out of him? Way. But what was freaking him out was that he wanted to shout to Laura how much he... What? How easily he could see himself still being with Laura beyond a season...or even two...or more?

A shiver ran up his spine despite the warm embrace and temperate dawn.

He couldn't believe *that* was in there trying to get out. Having thought it, he knew what his friends had each said was true. But there was no way he was ready to deal with a "keeper." He needed to tread very carefully here, this slope was filled with hotspots dying to reignite.

Akbar held Laura tighter for a moment, breathed her in for strength. "I've never been here before," he could admit that much without getting specific. "So let me sit with it for a minute and try not to run screaming into the woods."

"Don't do that," her bright laugh danced around him and made him feel lightheaded.

"Why?"

"Because you're naked, Fire Boy. And no, you can't have my blanket if you're going to go dragging it through the woods."

"Not even a corner of it?" Using his teeth, he slid it off her shoulder and nibbled on her bare skin.

"No." But she didn't try to tug the blanket back up.

"How about this little bit here?" he moved aside a flap with his nose and tipped her back to nuzzle the breast now glowing in the moonlight.

"Absolutely not!" Her breath was accelerating, going a bit gaspy. She gathered the blanket into her grasp and pulled it over her, around the back of his head.

Slowly, fold by fold, he maneuvered and shifted her in his lap until the blanket was around them rather than between them. And then, because the nearest protection was all the way in the bedroom, he made love to her with his mouth and his hands. He did it slowly, care-fully, and very thoroughly, dragging out the exquisite mutual torture until the sunrise forced him to leave this woman and this place where he could imagine a lifetime.

CHAPTER 8

"What's with you, Akbar?" Two-Tall was scraping the soil line to clear it of burnable fuel. The MHA Hoodies were working the line up in the Northern Cascades, just south of the Canadian border in northern nowhere Washington. They were working along the border cut through the heart of the Okanagan Forest, trying to fire proof it so that the approaching wildfire wasn't among the day's exports.

The border here lay down in the trees offering only narrow views to the east and west. They didn't have permission to do any felling where they normally would have on the far side of break. Americans cutting down Canadian timber was frowned on by the authorities, so they were preparing as well as they could to hold the line at the border. The terrain here was high, relatively flat, and almost wholly inaccessible by conventional equipment. So the smokies were on it.

Akbar kept his rhythm going. Nothing was showing, he was sure of that. He was right in sync with the rest of the crew. Ganged up in a line like this, they could clean a thirty-foot wide swath at the equivalent of a slow walk.

Krista set the line and used the wide flat blade of her Pulaski to drag three feet of loose surface crap, from left to right, past where she stood. Then she'd step forward and drag the next blade-width down the line. The team followed behind her stagger step, each moving the initial detritus another two to three feet away from the fire and then scraping their own section clear with a second stroke. By the time the pile reached Akbar and Tim at the end of the line, the bulk could be pretty substantial, but that's why they were the tail end of the line—the heavy lifters heaving everything as far as they could from the fire break's edge.

Tim, reading Akbar's silence as an excuse to continue his harangue did just that. "You been weird ever since we cleared Laura's woods a couple weeks back. You still good with her?"

"Yeah, we're still good." And they were. Mostly. Wanting to tell the woman he wanted to spend his life with her had shocked the hell out of him. He could feel the "L" word looming somewhere on the horizon like a single wisp of smoke promising imminent disaster. The "L" word was one reserved for mothers and sisters, like "Love you, Dipwad." It wasn't meant for women he was seeing.

Seeing.

He'd smack himself for that one if both of his hands weren't busy. "Seeing" is what you did with windsurfer babes. "Dating" is what you did in high school, except he hadn't. A couple of one-time movie dates with other Chess Club or Physics Club members didn't count as even that. He and Laura were...

And that's where he got stuck in his head every time.

Tim was on a roll, though keeping his voice low enough so only Akbar could hear it. He wasn't talking about the fire trying to burn a new passage from northern Washington into Canada, so Akbar did the best he could to tune him out. Last thing he needed to do was talk to Tim about his love life.

Damn it! There was that word again.

He clipped his boot with the edge of his Pulaski, putting a slice in the leather. Just that much sooner he'd be replacing these boots. Damn it to hell! He liked these boots.

Tim clunked him in the helmet with the butt of his axe. Akbar had moved too far forward, not waiting for his turn to move the scrap out of the fire break. He'd broken the rhythm of the line. The ripple went up the line with missed steps, awkward moves. The pace broke.

Krista, proving she was a smart leader, called a five-minute break by shouting, "Drink up. Fuel up."

Everyone sat where they were and dug into their personal gear bag for energy bars and water. Ox pulled out an MRE and began eating it cold. The high smoke was mostly blowing south, but the fire was flowing north following a gentle breeze and a generous fuel supply. The blue sky above the border cut belied the fire that was approaching from the south, but for the moment, it was peaceful and pretty. The choppers were fighting the battle well to the south and only rarely passed over their present position. He half expected Laura and her train of horses to show up out of the trees and flash one of those smiles at him.

But he'd seen less and less of that smile all week. Tim wasn't the only one sensing something was wrong. Akbar wished he knew what it was, he really did. He needed something he could reach out and fix. But he couldn't find it. He'd long since run out of places to look.

"Hi Jeannie."

"Hey Laura," the chopper pilot looked genuinely pleased to see her which she'd take as a good sign. "Akbar's still sacked out. That last fire was a long, hard slog for those guys."

"I figured." It was only Laura's second trip to the MHA airfield. Johnny had toured her around once, on a quiet day when almost no one was about. It was a lot livelier today even if the smokies were asleep. On the far side of the field, five helicopters stood in a line. There were two small ones, one of which was Jeannie's MD500, two mid-sized ones looking gawky with a long two-blade rotor, and the one big Firehawk. Service crews had the covers off the second one in the line.

"Something wrong?"

Jeannie followed her gaze, "No, Denise is doing periodic maintenance. She seems to think that us pilots actually using any of her precious aircraft is a sacrilege and that we're not to be trusted. She gives each bird a serious once-over after every fire. Can't complain because she always gets us in the air with no downtime."

Sure enough, Laura could see one of the team break off and move up to the next chopper. He had a tablet computer and was working his way down an electronic checklist as he moved about the chopper.

The two jump planes, parked beyond the choppers, had a cargo team going over chainsaws, sharpening axes, and testing the portable pumps using water from a fifty-five gallon drum perched on a forklift. A pair of small twin-engine planes sat at the end of the row, the Air Commander's plane and the lead plane to guide in the big air tankers.

"Chutes will be over in the loft repacking all of their parachutes. He has a couple riggers who go over every canopy and line each time. Can't even remember the last time someone had to pull a reserve chute. He jumped for twenty years before taking over the loft, so he's pretty rabid about perfection, too."

"Seems like you all are."

"That's what makes it work. We're lean here, a lot of cross-training, but for every ten pair of boots on the ground, we have two more here. And for every blade in the sky, we have three pairs of boots on the ground. Takes a lot to keep us running."

"What about—"

"You figured," Jeannie cut her off, "that Akbar was out cold, so I'm guessing you came to see me. You didn't come here to talk to me about firefighting."

Laura wanted to argue, but couldn't find any real point to it. Without her noticing, Jeannie had led her down the length of the field. Away from the bunkhouse where Johnny was sure to be sound asleep, they'd gotten back late last night—his *Sleep* text had come in after eleven. They wandered past the kitchen building and its friendly cluster of picnic tables where the crews obviously spent a lot of time.

At the far end of the field, they followed the course of a small stream that splashed and gurgled its way into the trees. About a hundred yards in, the stream slowed for a moment to form a wide pool. It was quiet here. No sense of the bustle going on beyond the trees.

"I don't really know you," Laura finally broke the easy silence as they sat on a fallen tree trunk and watched the water flow by, "but you were nice to me that day when they cleared my trees. I don't know why, Jeannie, but I feel I can trust you. Maybe because of how much Johnny likes you."

"There's nothing between—"

"I know that or I wouldn't have come here. That's not what this is about."

Jeannie nodded for her to continue.

Laura had practiced this in her head while working up the courage to come here. She didn't know Jeannie. They'd sat back-to-back at the Doghouse but hadn't spoken. Jeannie had hovered overhead for almost fifteen minutes while Johnny rescued Grayson Masterson, but Johnny had done all of the radio work.

Their whole acquaintance consisted of barely speaking during a the crew's scrutiny into her viability as the love interest of the much beloved Akbar the Great.

"You're talking yourself out of asking your question, aren't you?"

She glanced over at Jeannie then offered a sigh and smile. "Yes. How did you know?"

"Do it myself all the time. Takes one to know one." Then Jeannie bumped her shoulder against Laura's. "Just ask. Right now before you actually succeed."

"What's wrong?" Laura gasped out a breath, then laughed. "Who ever thought two words could be so hard to say. Not quite how I rehearsed it."

"You're asking me for top secret disclosures about a good friend of mine?"

"I guess. Sounds kinda stupid, doesn't it?"

"Well," Jeannie pried up a bit of bark from the log they were perched on and winged it into the pool.

A Stellar jay so proud in his blue feathered coat had settled on the far side of the stream to take a drink. He now squawked and flapped off in a huff, stopping briefly in a nearby tree to complain bitterly before finally departing.

"I wish I could help."

"But you can't because he's your friend," Laura tried to mask her disappointment, but knew she didn't succeed well. "I understand."

"I can't," Jeannie poked her in the arm making her look up, "because I haven't a clue. Johnny has something stuck in his craw, we can all see it. He's even got Tim worried, which is hard to do. He's pretty unflappable."

"What's stuck in there?"

"My best guess," Jeannie smiled kindly, "is you."

"Oh great. And what am I supposed to do about that?"

Jeannie shook her head and they went back to pitching bits of dead tree into the stream.

"HEY, TIM?" Akbar lay wide awake on his bunk.

"Huh?" Two-Tall grunted from the upper bunk.

"You awake?"

"No!"

"Sorry. Go back to sleep." Akbar considered kicking the mattress above him to wake Tim the rest of the way up.

"Oh man," Tim groaned. "Now is when you gotta to talk? Not on the line? Not on the flight back? What is it, three in the morning?"

"More like eight-thirty," though the blackout curtains kept the room dark. Nothing to see except the vague outlines of a standing dresser and a small bookcase they'd managed to wedge into the corner of the small space. They were both voracious and eclectic readers, which had been their bond from the first day.

"And you've been awake since... Shit." There was no real heat behind the sleepy curse. "Well, I'm awake now. Hit me with it."

Akbar didn't know how to start. It was all a jumble in his head no matter how much he thought about it.

"You ever gotten serious, Tim? About a girl?"

"Sure," Tim managed around a yawn. "You've seen Steve's classic Firebird. That girl is so cherry. I could get really serious about driving her."

"Crap, Tim! I'm talking about—"

"Laura, I know. Your sense of humor has gone to hell since you started with her, you know that don't you?"

He didn't.

"In answer to your stupid-ass question, what does my level of serious have to do with anything to a man already standing in the middle of the flame?"

"What do you mean?"

The bunk shifted as Tim rolled over. He could see the vague outline of Tim's head as he looked down at Akbar over the edge.

"You left serious behind a while ago, buddy." It was the kindest tone he'd ever heard from Tim. "Sooner you admit to that shit, the happier you'll be."

"I don't—"

"Crap, Akbar! How did she fall for you rather than me? Can you tell me that one?"

"Must be my good looks and superior character!" His sense of humor damn well wasn't dead and he could give back as good as he got.

"Idiot! She fell for *you,* thickhead. Not because of any of that normal crap. Not because you're a smokie. Not that you're crew boss and not because you're actually a funny guy when you're not being quite so dumb. It's *you* she wants. Now what you need to do is figure out how to be yourself around her and let the rest of us sleep in peace." Tim flopped back onto his bunk. By the way the bed moved, he was digging back in to go back to sleep.

Himself? He was supposed to be himself?

He squinted up at the square-pattern of springs across the bottom of the mattress above him, but he couldn't see it.

Be himself?

Who the hell was that?

"BUT HE'S DRIFTING AWAY," Laura indicated the latest bit of moss-coated bark Jeannie had tossed on the pool. This time the Stellar jay ignored them entirely as it started bathing on the far side of the pool with head dips and wing flutters in the clear shallow water.

The big of moss clung to its tiny boat as it slowly bobbed its way toward the pool's outlet where the stream would soon whisk it away. "I don't know how to pull him back from wherever he's going."

"I'm not so sure you can pull someone like Akbar back once he's headed down a road."

"Wow!" Laura felt the tightness in her throat and chest but refused to give in to it. "That cheers me up no end."

"Okay," Jeannie admitted, "that didn't come out quite the way I intended."

"Duh!"

"Let me try again. No…" Jeannie worried at her lower lip for a moment and Laura felt better for seeing that.

"No," she started again. "I going to stick with that statement. Once he's headed down *a* road—not as in *the* road, like he's gone—then… I didn't mean that. He's…" she squinted her eyes at the pool as she searched for the right words.

So Laura squinted as well. "He's looking for what's stuck in his craw, but he doesn't know what it is?"

"Right," Jeannie turned to her with a bright smile. "Until he saw you, his life made sense. Ah, especially the women in his life made sense. He—" She cut herself off.

"It's okay. Remember, I first met Johnny and Tim at the Doghouse."

"Yeah, they are pretty sweet when they think they're being subtle. But I'll tell you what, Laura. Whatever you did to him those ten minutes or so he was at your table, wasn't like any version of Akbar I've ever seen before. You changed him, right there. That fast."

Laura had to sit with that one a moment. She watched the Stellar finish its bath, then inspect her for a long moment before flitting off into the woods. Now only the sounds of the trickling water filled the air.

She'd never had that effect on any guy. She actually was, what had Tim called it, *a catch-and-release type*. At least that's how men had always treated her. That's all Grayson Masterson had wanted. A diversion, a conquest, and no more.

"You really did. I've known him for four years. I think you've already set a longevity record and certainly maxed out his confusion meter."

Laura swallowed hard. Did she want him badly enough to fight for him? If she was being honest, that wasn't even a question.

"Any suggestions?" she couldn't bring herself to look up as the latest bit of bark reached the end of the pool, was sucked downstream, and instantly shot out of sight.

"Only one that I can think of."

Jeannie's silence forced Laura to look up at her. She had a slow, goofy smile on her face.

"What?"

"Do nothing different at all."

"That's advice?" Laura couldn't do that. The risk of losing such an amazing man was too great. She had to… What?

"That's advice," Jeannie nodded to herself. "Maybe the best advice I've ever given."

"Is this one of those set-them-free-and-if-they-love-you-they'll-come back lessons?"

"Nope. At least I didn't mean it to be." Jeannie's smile had grown huge. "He's used to women getting clingy or pissed off. He has pre-built, field-tested methods of dealing with every form of woman who thinks there is more there than was promised. I bet he doesn't have a single tool in his entire personal arsenal to deal with a woman who simply loves him for who he is. Especially not how to get rid of her when deep down he doesn't want to."

Laura studied Jeannie's grinning face, watched the water, looked for the jay, and then looked back to Jeannie's grin. Then she started to laugh. If being herself had snared the man's attention and now totally confounded him, what in the world would he do with a woman who was learning how to stay herself?

It was a hell of a gamble.

Jeannie's laugh matched her own. Which didn't go hysterical. Instead, it was truly funny. For once she was confusing the hell out of a man instead of the other way around.

She reached out to hug Jeannie and the woman hugged her back.

Now she hoped to god it worked.

That's when an eerie sound rose to fill the woods.

"FIRE!" Akbar shouted as he rolled to the foot of his bunk before swinging out his feet. Two-Tall jumped to the floor right beside him.

The fire siren roared up into its howling whine until everyone in the whole complex was up and preparing for action. As the two of them dragged on their long cotton underwear, stuffed feet into unlaced boots, and grabbed jumpsuits, he could hear other sets of feet hitting floorboards all down the hall. All around them, smokies were gearing up to fight fire. Fifteen minutes from first call to takeoff was the goal, and MHA hadn't been late once all summer.

He and Two-Tall were the first into the hall. No need to pound on doors. Krista stumbled out in front of him, sports bra still showing as she tried to get dressed, walk, and drag along her jumpsuit. She careened into a wall. Two-Tall tickled her ribs as they slipped past. Krista squirmed and cursed, too snarled up and asleep to retaliate.

The smokies were among the first to gather in the area below the control tower. Though the ground crew and pilots weren't far behind. Betsy, the camp cook, and her assistant started working the crowd with a pitcher of coffee, a stack of to-go cups, and a basket of bagels.

That's when Akbar saw her, exactly as he'd pictured her at their very first meeting.

Laura came running out of the woods two paces ahead of Jeannie. He long auburn hair streaming out behind her. Her long legs making her sprint look smooth and effortless. The morning sunlight caught her hair as she moved out of the trees' shadows and struck her as if she'd been lit by fire.

Damn woman glowed with an impossible magic. No. This was Laura Judith Jenson. She glowed like she'd been beamed down to the planet from some vastly superior and more brilliant world.

He was stunned speechless as he watched her. She spotted him and trotted to a smooth stop right in front of him. She was beyond beautiful. She was—

"Good morning, lover," her tone soft and private. Then she kissed him. Kissed him until his whole crew was hooting and hollering at them. She pulled back enough to speak. "Go kick some fire butt for me!"

Then she flashed one of those killer smiles at him, winked at Jeannie for reasons passing understanding, and trotted away toward the parking lot as Mark climbed the stairs to launch them at the latest fire, wherever it was.

He watched her go until she was out of sight, then whispered to himself.

"I am so screwed."

"You got that right, brother." Tim slapped a meaty hand down on his shoulder. And for the first time, Akbar actually went down to his knees under the blow. Tim dragged him back up to his feet by the harness of his jumpsuit.

CHAPTER 9

*L*aura *wanted to abandon* the plan dozens of times over the next few weeks. At first she didn't because she couldn't think of a better one. Also, she didn't like the image of herself as a desperate woman. So, she maintained her vigil as: welcoming lover, morning run companion, and someone who simply liked Johnny without judgment. She laughed at Johnny's jokes—at least the funny ones, shared his silences, and did her best not to buy into his own personal turmoil.

She'd expected to go through her own cycle of fear, uncertainty, and doubt, but it didn't come up for her. The more she was around Johnny, the more herself she became. Tim had been right, she wasn't the catch-and-release type; she was the constant-and-steady type. Once Johnny had proven to her that she was worthy of his on-going attentions, she—ridiculous as it sounded—become worthy of them. At least she hoped so.

If she thought too hard about it all, it stopped making sense. But if she unfocused her brain as if she were in that dreamy state that occurred deep into a long, lazy trail ride, all of the pieces slid together for her. She loved Johnny, pretty desperately. He loved her, but he was having a hard time accepting that.

Jeannie's plan was right. Just keep loving him and work at being her truest self. Then, hopefully, if they were indeed meant for each other, he'd arrive at that same conclusion.

It hurt her to watch his struggles, but she couldn't think of how to step in and ease them without getting too invasive. And whatever was going on, he wasn't ready to talk about it yet. When she pushed, he merely looked sad and worried; she didn't want to do that to him.

There were times she had to close her own pain off until he went to another fire, or even back to MHA for the day. She didn't let it show, or didn't think that she did. But once he was gone, she'd sometimes curl up around his pillow and cry for his anguish.

Even though Johnny might be going quietly nuts, he kept coming back to her arms. He wanted to be with her no matter how he fought against it. And for now that's what counted.

When he had a free day he'd join her up at the Lodge, equally content to be hiking the hills or watching the birds. He proved himself as able to learn horsemanship as to learn walking on crampons.

There was one holdout though. No matter what bribe he offered, Mister Ed still had little use for him. At first she'd felt bad for Johnny and tried to bridge whatever the gap might be. But then she began to be amused by his growing perplexity. It obviously rankled deeply that he couldn't win over the horse.

"Maybe he thinks you smell like a forest fire and that scares him," Laura had tried easing another awkward rejection. Awkward on Johnny's part; she had to fight to not laugh as he leaned on the corral fence at the Lodge and glared at the horse.

"No. This is guy stuff. He thinks I'm after his woman."

"Are you?" she couldn't help teasing, doing her best to not let the serious question behind the tease show through.

"Was Paris hot for Helen?"

"What?" sometimes his references were too obscure, though she got the feeling that she caught more than most.

"Paris, the cocky ass Prince who sacrificed his entire city so that he could bed that fair but faithless minx Helen of Troy."

"So..." Laura liked the way that sounded, "you'd sacrifice a city for me?"

"Sure. As long as you don't make it too big a one."

"Cheapskate!" She stuck her tongue out at him.

"Nope, just lazy," he'd lounged back against the fence and looked at her in a way that made her very sorry she had a hike scheduled to start in a few minutes. "How about Hood River? I could sacrifice the town of Hood River for you."

"Oh, we're down to mere towns now? You promised me a city. Besides, you'd never lay waste to the Doghouse Inn."

"True. True. How about Spokane? No one would miss it, I mean not really. It's in a whole other state for crying out loud."

"Deal!" They shook on it. They'd parted with a kiss that was as sweet as ever and had her practically skipping like a schoolgirl on her way to the Lodge to meet the guests.

When she'd glanced back from the last turn that would hide the corral, he still stood there, studying the horse rather than watching her.

Yep, she was stuck in his craw but good and he still didn't see it. At some point soon he was going to either choke on it, or spit her out as too much trouble.

She decided that it was time to put a mark on her calendar. One more week and she would have spent a month being tolerant of the man who so wanted to be with her, but couldn't stop looking for a reason to run away.

That would be enough. If he didn't have his act together by then, she'd be the one to break the relationship silence. Because except for this one tiny flaw, Johnny was daily becoming more and more the man of her dreams.

CHAPTER 10

Out on the trail, Laura dismissed the first hint of the fire when she tasted it on the wind. Johnny often missed a spot during his shower, or wore his jump boots out to the cabin. He smelled like many things that were wonderful, but one of them that lurked about him as often as not was wood smoke.

Mister Ed rolled easily along the Skyline Trail, six tourists close behind on this easy section. It was fully melted out and was going to make a great two-day ride. The Pacific Crest National Scenic Trail, commonly called the PCT, ran from the Mexican border to Canada along some of the harshest wilderness that the Sierra Nevadas and the Cascades could hand out.

The PCT climbed from river to snowline and back down to river time and again in brutal elevation changes. She'd always meant to hike or ride its length. So far she'd covered all of the Oregon portion and most of Washington. California beckoned. Maybe she'd been unconsciously waiting for the right companion.

At Mount Hood the PCT followed the Skyline Trail that skirted the late summer snowline from above Timberline Lodge. It passed along the southern and western glaciers before wandering off towards the Columbia Gorge and the Bridge of the Gods. By adding in a loop with some great views on the first day, it made for a long afternoon's ride to reach the primitive shelter at Paradise Park which was actually only a few lazy hours' ride away. It allowed for a straight shot back after breakfast gave them time for a shower before lunch.

Sometimes Laura would extend the ride over to Burnt Lake or a sweet little meadow she'd found on Slide Mountain, but that took more skilled riders. Not this crowd. This time she had two sets of newlyweds, all four of them game, but none of them up for anything trickier than an easy trot. The group was rounded out by a mother-daughter team who were celebrating their mutual graduation from college; mom had gone back to school for teaching marine science when her daughter had started in pre-med. They rode well enough, but were simply having too good a time together for the destination to be of any real importance, as long as they were doing it together.

Laura spent a while daydreaming about children. About her children. She'd like a girl. Not that there'd be any pressure, but she was an only child. If there was going to be a fourth generation of the matrilineal line of Jenson trail guides, it was going to be up to her.

She couldn't resist the smile. There was a sure way to blow all of Johnny's gaskets. "Hi honey. So how many kids do you want to have? Let's not wait."

"Poof!" she said it softly, the sound of Johnny's brain exploding like a dandelion gone to seed moments before a hurricane hit. Yes, one thing at a time. First she had to wait for Johnny to—

Mister Ed slowed to a halt and dropped his ears back.

Laura didn't try to force him ahead; he was a very trail-wise horse. She scanned the trail ahead for rattlesnakes. Very rare at this altitude in this area, but she looked. Bear were more likely, but she could hear no telltale crash and thump through the twenty- and thirty-foot firs that grew in the area; bears rarely moved quietly. The world was very quiet.

Mister Ed's reaction was wrong for elk or deer; he was as likely to want to go play with them as anything else.

Then she caught that hint of wood smoke again. The lightest of afternoon breezes was cool against her sun-warmed face, slipping down off the glaciers in gentle wafts of ice-scented air. But there was…

The rest of the group had come to a stop behind her. She turned slowly in her saddle scanning farther afield for the cause.

Smoke. A little thread of it. The fire was either small… No, she saw heat ripples to the south and the west. It was hot. So hot that there was little ash yet. The breeze shifted for a moment and she caught it again. Wood smoke.

Mister Ed snorted.

Laura pulled out her radio. All she could pull in was static. She couldn't reach the Lodge because there was now half a mountain between them. No rangers responded to her call either. Not even the ski patrol that would be high up on Palmer. They'd come too far around the mountain's curve.

Maybe they'd come far enough.

Johnny had given her MHA's direct frequency.

The voice that answered was harsh and rippling with static and squelch cutouts. She adjusted her own squelch setting and tried again.

"This is Laura Jenson. We have a fire on the west side of Mount Hood. It is around the five thousand foot level and climbing toward Zigzag Canyon."

She thought the crackling voice said something about ten minutes. Laura tucked away her radio and turned back to the group.

"Okay folks. I'm sorry to do this to you, but… Can you see the smoke starting down there below us?"

They all turned to look the direction she was indicating. The fire had found enough fuel that the smoke was now starting to show clearly.

"It's unlikely that it will develop into anything and I've already called it in. But for our own safety, I'm going to abort today's ride. What we'll do is turn around and head back toward the Lodge. The wildland firefighters are based just ten minutes away. They're on their way to check out the smoke and will let us know if we should continue back to the Lodge, or if we can turn around again and continue our ride. So we may be doubling back and forth a bit, but better safe than sorry, right?"

Everyone agreed. It took a little doing as they were in a relatively narrow portion of the trail, but they got their horses turned around. Once they were all set, she led them back into the long vertical slice of a canyon that the ice and water had carved down the face of the mountain. The fire she could see was traveling along the ridge they had just departed, and she didn't want to be anywhere near that.

The other horses in the group finally caught the occasional wind shifts of a sudden warm updraft laced with firesmoke from downslope. Ears went back, nerves went up.

She started teaching the group an old Brewer and Shipley song based on a Native American chant. It leant itself to a multi-part harmony that was easy even for the untrained. The song distracted the tourists and at the same time calmed their mounts.

Now if it would only distract her. They'd descended back into the trees and wouldn't re-emerge for over a mile. She didn't like riding blind with a fire so near.

AKBAR WAS HUNCHED over a breakfast of a tall stack of Betsy's killer blueberry pancakes, ham, and two eggs over easy. It was about what the other smokies who'd struggled out of their bunks were eating. Most of them were up and about except for the real sluggards who could sleep twelve hours at a stretch with little motivation. It was actually early afternoon lunch time, but Betsy was great about shifting meals to match when people woke up.

The picnic tables that were MHA's main gathering area were comfortable from the warming of the morning sun, but shielded from the midday heat by the kitchen and equipment buildings to the south. In the afternoon, the tall Doug firs to the west would offer sun-dappled shade. It was a good place to be.

They'd just come off two days on a fire, a small but intense blaze in northern California. They'd trapped it between a lake and a community that had actually maintained their urban-forest interface. They'd lost a couple of garden sheds, but no homes. A job well done and the local engine company had taken over yesterday shortly before dark.

Now they were up and relaxed. Ox was teasing Chas about not benching his own body weight when he did workouts; the fact that he could do more reps of a hundred pounds than Ox could was casually waved aside as meaningless. Krista and Tim were trying to get together a volleyball game for after breakfast, lunch, or whatever this was.

Akbar was enjoying the scene. He wished Laura was here. It was one of those good moments. The crew was rested, sitting easy. There'd been no injuries all season worse than Chas' sprained ankle and wrist. No bad burns at all. And they'd been able to respond to almost eighty percent of the fires they were called on—only a twenty percent "unable to be filled" rate. There were never enough resources and it wasn't at all unusual to be requested to a fire when the team was already deeply involved in another one. But only missing twenty percent meant they were kicking ass this season, in 2012 the UTF was over forty-five percent.

He looked around to assess the team. MHA kept a dozen of them year-round, which was very unusual. With most outfits, he'd have been lucky to keep Tim, Krista, and Ox full-time. But even his newest seasonal firefighter had five years on the line and two years jumping smoke. MHA's salaries and up-to-date equipment attracted the very best. Damn good crew.

Rumor had it that they'd be jumping Australia for a couple months this winter, which could be a nice change. Part of the price to keep them full-time, they'd have to travel to where the fires were. Maybe Laura could fly in for part of that and they could dive the Great Barrier Reef together or something like that.

Yeah, right. Long range plans with a woman. He could feel himself screwing up no matter how he was fighting against his own worst nature. Someday soon the most amazing woman he'd ever met would lower the boom on his sorry head. He'd deserve it too. He was clueless how to really do this and he knew it.

He forced himself to keep eating, he desperately needed the calories after two days on the fire line, but he wasn't enjoying it any longer. Why did things go sour every time he thought of her?

Like that stupid horse of hers. Every time he saw Mister Ed, he imagined how Laura looked riding him; that easy, confidant sway of a truly skilled rider. She made many things look easy, but her work with the horse was flawless. But no matter what good thoughts he tried to raise each time he looked at Mister Ed, the horse knew he didn't have his shit together.

A sharp whoosh and buzz overhead had most of the smokies glancing upward. Steve's drone launched and shot by overhead, then turned sharply south. Most returned to their breakfast, barely breaking their conversation.

Akbar glanced around. No Steve of course, he'd be at the drone's controls in his truck parked by the launcher. Might be a fire, might be a Search-and-Rescue, might be an equipment test.

No Carly at any of the tables either. Was she keeping her fiancé company or was she with him because there might be a fire?

No Henderson.

Akbar rose to his feet, took his tray to the wash bins. He rolled the remains of two pancakes around the ham and eggs like a massive and sloppy burrito. He trapped it between English muffins for a handhold, and headed over to Steve's control trailer. He did his best to appear casual to not alarm the others just in case it was nothing.

Around the backside of the bunkhouse where Steve kept his drone's service truck and launch trailer parked, they were all clustered together: Steve in the truck at his controls, Carly, Mark, TJ, and Emily grouped at the tailgate. They were waiting...waiting for the drone to get where it was going.

Akbar sidled up to the group, "What's happening?" He knew that if he asked, "What's up?" someone was bound to gaze uncertainly overhead and reply, "Blue sky." One of the many legacies he'd managed to instill in the MHA lexicon of humor. He took a big bite of his pancake burrito and managed not to wear any of the egg that was dripping out the back end and onto the grass.

Henderson answered him. "We got a badly broken radio report of a fire up on Mount Hood. Southwest we think. Rangers haven't reported anything yet. Steve's sending a drone to check it out."

Akbar felt his blood run a little cold. "Southwest?"

"Maybe she said west. It was hard to tell."

"She?" That cold chill turned into a deep freeze. Laura was leading a group ride today. They were supposed to overnight near the timberline on the West side. "Was it Laura?"

"Laura?" Henderson searched around a bit. "Oh, is that the lady who gave you the smacker of a kiss on the line the other day?"

"That's her."

Henderson shrugged. "You don't introduce me to a beautiful woman, I'm not going to recognize her voice. It was almost all static anyway. She sounded calm."

"Yeah, she's good at that," Akbar thought about it. Laura always sounded calm, even the few times he'd caught her red-eyed and choked up—something she'd never explained. And he'd been dumb enough to not ask about it the second time after the way she refused to explain it the first time. His policy was not to question crying women, ever. But for Laura he should have. Next time he would.

He chucked the rest of his meal in a handy garbage can and tried to settle in to wait. At ninety miles an hour, it took the drone over ten minutes to swing around Mount Hood's flank.

"We definitely have a fire," Steve announced.

"Where's Laura?"

"I don't even know where the fire is yet. Give me a minute." Steve kept one of his monitors twisted to the side so that they could see it as they crowded around the tailgate. The sides of Mount Hood were practically corrugated by long ridges running from peak to valley all around its slopes.

The smoke was spreading along either side of a long canyon that separated two long ridges. That was good. It meant there'd be water they could pump right from the stream running down the center of the canyon.

"You've got to find Laura," he told Steve.

Steve tapped quickly at some keys, "There, I've configured the drone as a relay." He handed a microphone to Henderson, but Akbar grabbed it without bothering to ask or apologize.

"Laura, this is Johnny." He ignored the surprised looks the others aimed his way. "Can you hear me, over?"

"HEY JOHNNY AKBAR THE GREAT." Laura was so happy to hear his voice. She could definitely taste the smoke on the air now, though the sky that she could see straight above was still clear of smoke. But it wasn't all that much blue through the narrow slice of trees.

"Where are you, Laura?"

"Almost directly below Paradise Park, down in Zigzag Canyon. At the moment we're heading back for the Lodge. We're fine. We're watering the horses at the stream along the Pacific Crest Trail." *Watering them to keep them calm,* she didn't add because she didn't want her group of tourists to hear that. The horses were getting twitchy and the cool spring water serve as only a momentary distraction. She wasn't sure if they could get out of this canyon without the horses bolting and their riders were definitely not skilled enough to deal with that.

There was a long silence. She began counting her own heartbeats and passed twenty so quickly that she stopped counting.

"We're trying to find you," Johnny called back. "Could you do me a favor? Transmit a count to thirty nice and slow. Start now."

His request didn't make a lot of sense, but she did as he asked. While she was counting aloud, she assessed the group. The tourists were still thinking this was all a part of a good story for them to tell at home. None of them were aware of how uneasy their mounts were becoming. The horses' nostrils and ears were working hard, but it also meant that the horses weren't trying to grab every passing berry bush so their inexperienced riders were actually having an easier time of it.

Then she heard it. A small engine circling overhead. She tried to catch a glimpse of it. It sounded like a small and quiet lawnmower, not a helicopter. Through a gap in the trees she spotted a flicker of a black shape against the sky.

Laura knew it instantly. It was the same type of drone her father built up in Hood River. She'd forgotten about that first meal with Johnny and her parents. He'd called over a couple who then talked to her father about using drones on wildfires. MHA had one of her father's special drones. It must be homing in on her radio signal.

Near the end of her count, it flashed by close above her. It might have even waggled its wings before disappearing from view behind a tree.

"THE FIRE'S WRONG," Carly said it softly, but with no question in her voice as Laura's count was coming in over the radio and Steve was doing whatever he did with radio signals to pinpoint their location.

Akbar looked at it again. The smoke was billowing up, indicating that the winds weren't too turbulent yet. The fire itself was traveling upslope which was natural, especially in the light wind conditions.

Crap! It was burning upslope...from several areas of the mountain's flank all at once. They were actually separate blazes in the process of joining into a single fire as they moved upslope ready to sweep over the mountain's flank. There were only two ways to start a fire like this one.

A campfire, cigarette butt, and most other human causes that accounted for eighty percent of all wildfires had a single point of origin. A multi-point origin could be caused by a lightning strike. He glanced up at the cloudless blue sky as Laura finished her count.

"Okay, we have you," he had to work hard to keep his voice calm as he answered her. "Give us a sec." He clicked off the radio.

The second way to get a wildfire with a multi-point origin was human caused. Intentionally human caused. Arson.

Steve zoomed in the view. He'd flipped to infrared to show the seven tightly clustered heat dots of tourists on horseback deep in the trees.

"This is the Skyline Trail," Steve overlaid the line on the map. The line passed right through the clustered group continuing side to side across the mountain's flank, dipping into canyons and climbing over ridges.

Akbar took one look at Henderson then keyed the microphone.

"Laura?"

"Yes, Johnny?"

"Listen carefully. This is really important. Do *not* move from where you are. No matter what, you stay by that creek. We're coming to get you."

He heaved the mike aside and sprinted back around the bunkhouse to roust his crew. The others followed close on his heels. He did his best to not think about the image on the screen.

Where it climbed out of Zigzag Canyon in either direction, the Pacific Crest Trail was already on fire atop the ridges. And a new fire was starting the long crawl up the center of the canyon.

CHAPTER 11

Laura had everybody dismount. It had taken almost fifteen minutes for the drone to find them from when she'd first placed the call. Fifteen more and she'd have a bunch of tourists bucked to the ground.

"Okay everybody, listen up." Laura wished Johnny had explained what was going on, but he hadn't. And his voice had done its dead calm, soothing thing that he did so well. And, quite frankly, that was really, really freaking her out at the moment. But the tourists didn't know that. Johnny was being very smart. As usual.

"We're going to wait here for a bit."

"It's getting kind of smoky." "Aren't we going back to the Lodge?" "Can we—"

She raised her hands to stop all of the questions. She took a deep breath and pulled out her best trail-guide-serious tone, rather than the trail-guide-upbeat one she'd been attempting to maintain.

"We have been asked by a team of wildland firefighters to remain in our current position. Did anyone notice the small drone that flew overhead?"

Some had. Some hadn't.

"They have a much better idea of what's going around us that we possibly could. They're the very best."

It was the pre-med student daughter who put it together first. "This isn't some campfire that we're smelling? This is a..." she swallowed hard and then whispered it, "...a forest fire?"

The tension in the group ratcheted up about ten levels.

"I'd say that's a real possibility." So this is how Johnny did it. She could feel the change inside herself. Over the years she'd dealt with injuries, frostbite, hunger, snakebites, and a hundred other emergencies. She'd never dealt with a forest fire. Yet she'd found a place inside her that could remain the calm center no matter what she was feeling.

That's how Johnny fought forest fires no matter how he'd been feeling over the last month. And that's how he'd gone so long without speaking to her. His fear was locked tightly deep inside and—at least to everyone else in the world—he appeared calm and in control.

It wasn't a lesson she particularly wanted to have at the moment, but for now she'd latch onto it and hope she was alive in the morning to figure out how to help.

"What we're going to do is remain calm."

"Remain calm?!" One of the newlyweds was not impressed with the idea. Gus, one of the guys.

"Yes. For two reasons. One is that if we panic, then the horses will panic. In this terrain that would be very dangerous for the horses and possibly for us as well." Zigzag Canyon led up between steep rocky walls until it hit the Zigzag Glacier. Any horse attempting to climb off the trail was bound to break a leg. And heading down the canyon... Well, she'd wager that wasn't a good idea at the moment or Johnny wouldn't have been so worried.

"The second reason," she said in as calm a voice as possible, "is that the person who told us to stay put is the very best smokejumper in the business. His own team calls him Akbar the Great because he really is that great against fire. I would trust his advice over anyone's on the planet."

That did the job. At least for now. The group was calming down.

Laura glanced at the thin strip of blue showing above the trees, then quickly turned her attention back to the circle of expectant faces hoping none of them looked up.

"Now what we have to do is keep the horses calm, because they don't understand why we're merely standing here when they think we should be running. I want everyone to take out those Timberline Lodge t-shirts I handed out this morning. I'll get you new ones. Tuck them into the top of the horses' bridles so that it covers their eyes and most of their nose, but not their nostrils."

"What they can't see won't hurt them?" The mom found her sense of humor. Laura could hug the woman.

"Right." She considered tying the horses together into a train, but decided against it. If they did have to run for it and one was injured, Laura didn't want to risk losing all the others.

She did her best to keep the group busy at tending the horses so that she wouldn't have to think too much.

When no one was watching, she stole another glance skyward. Her thin strip of blue hope high above the trees was turning ash and smoke gray.

THE FIRE WAS SO close and the need so urgent, they didn't bother with the parachutes or the planes. Akbar had his crews fully geared up and on the Firehawk and one of the 212s in under five minutes. Emily and Jeannie had them aloft by five minutes and one second. Six more minutes to reach the canyon at full throttle. Eleven minutes. Eleven of the slowest minutes in his life.

He dragged on a headset and spoke into the microphone on the air attack frequency. There had been fifteen of the twenty-four smokies at the camp, so they were split five and ten between the choppers. Vern was already loading up the rest of the smokies into the other 212 medium-lift Huey helicopter. Jeannie patched Akbar through to Emily's bird where he knew Krista would be repeating his instructions to the larger team as he said them.

"We're going in helitack. Everyone make sure your descenders are properly attached on your own harness and your buddy's." He screamed silently at his desperation to rush even faster to Laura's side, but kept his voice steady.

Evans, the backender who climbed aboard to assist Jeannie, rigged rope lines to extender arms that slid out the top of the cargo bay door. They were little more than a bar with a steel loop on the end. A line tied to the loop would dangle a foot beyond the cargo bay door—easy to reach and pull aboard to run through the descender device attached to each smokie's harness. Evans would throw a line out either side of the cargo bay when they were over the drop site.

The crew checked their descenders and gathered their gear. They'd be going in heavy with chainsaws, axes, and pumps. He wanted to throw the whole team into the canyon. He wanted to build a wall of smokies around Laura. But that wasn't the right answer.

"Krista, your crew goes in on the top of the ridge to the east. Ox, Chas, and Patrick are going onto the ridge to the west. The rest of the smokies coming in Vern's bird will join you in a few minutes. Tim, you're down in the canyon with me."

"There it is," Jeannie whispered over the intercom.

Akbar leaned out the open cargo bay door to see. The fire was building. The flames were no longer down in the undergrowth, they were starting to snap into the air above the treetops. He did his best to visualize the points of origin so that he could estimate the fire's path of travel. All he could see was the clump of trees where Laura must be trapped.

There were many situations that a firefighter didn't want to get into. One of the most dangerous was in between two heads of running fire. There was a desire to get between them so that you could fight the battle on two fronts from a single position. But it was one of the most dangerous mistakes you could make because there could be no escape route if the two heads merged.

That's where Laura and her people were.

"Okay," he returned his attention to the attack plan. "This is an extract." The safest method would be to take down harnesses and lift the tourists out on winches. But because of the depth of the canyon and the height of the surrounding trees, the choppers would have to stay at least eighty feet in the air. Probably three minutes per winch run: lower the wire to the ground, get the tourist snapped in, winched up, and back off the cable once inside the chopper. Seven people, twenty-one minutes. Wasn't going to work.

"Rig more lines, Evans. Be sure to stagger-step the lengths. We're going short-haul."

"Akbar," Jeannie spoke up, "with tourists? You can't do that."

"Burnover of their position is under thirty minutes. If you have a better idea, I'm open to it." That came out far harsher than he intended. "Sorry, Jeannie. Let's drop Ox and his crew first."

He could hear her reluctant consent even though she didn't say a word. And she was right, they were right out on the edge of the safety envelope, which was never a good idea.

"Okay people. Let's keep our heads about us. We're the MHA smokies. We're chill, we're good, and we get it done. Number one priority is safety. I don't want so much as a broken fingernail on this one. We clear on that, Krista?"

"Up yours, Akbar," was her friendly reply over the radio.

"Let's do it!"

Jeannie pulled them to halt. Out the cargo bay window, he could barely see Emily on the far side of the canyon through the smoke haze. Tiny black dots began dropping down lines too thin to see at this distance. They looked as if they were falling, but not gaining speed. *Smooth and steady, team!* he sent the thought to follow them down.

With the ease of long practice, his own crew was also dropping rapidly. One by one the smokies reached out to grab the rope hanging from just above the door. They pulled it in, slipped the rope into their descender brake, and a buddy would double-check it. Then they'd move to sit on the edge of the cargo bay decking with their feet dangling over thin air. With a final check by Tim, they'd lean out letting the line take their weight, dangle for a moment, and then slide downward out of sight. The next one moved into position in the door and began preparing to do the same as soon as their teammate hit the ground and got off the rope.

When there were only the two of them left, Jeannie began moving the chopper down into the canyon. Evans had snapped pairs of harnesses onto the ends of the ropes and now tossed the ends out the doors.

Before they descended into the haze, Akbar saw the smaller choppers arrive and Henderson's Incident Command plane appeared high overhead. They'd know to protect the group down in the canyon first and then worry about the fire's spread second.

He snapped his descender brake onto the line and waited for Jeannie to get them in position over Laura's group. Tim readied himself on the other side of the cargo bay. They'd go out opposite doors together.

Tim reached across to lay a hand on Akbar's shoulder. Whether it was to communicate encouragement or to keep Akbar in place until Jeannie was fully positioned, he wasn't sure.

LAURA HAD HEARD the arrival of the choppers, practically holding her breath for the two minutes they were maneuvering above but still out of sight.

The horses were actively snorting, but the t-shirt blinds were sufficient so far. The tourists were starting to look really worried. It wasn't quite time to dampen cloths for the humans to breathe through, but it was close. She'd been on the verge of having to knock down one of the guys to keep him from bolting up the trail. The need had been allayed when the canyon filled with the unmistakable pounding sound of a heavy chopper moving into position above them.

She looked up and saw a pair of smokies were sliding down the ropes. Despite their full gear, their contrast in height made it clear that it was Johnny and Tim. She actually cried out in relief.

In moments Johnny was on the ground and in her arms. Helmet, fire clothes, axe, harness…she didn't care. He felt wonderful, for the single moment she allowed herself to hang onto him.

"Good to see you, Space Ace."

"Good to see you, Fire Boy." She did her best not to weep, though she could feel the tears running hot down her cheeks.

Johnny turned to the tourists after offering her one of his encouraging smiles. "Well folks, we're going to send you on an adventure that none of you had expected today. Today you get to do something that few people ever do outside of wildland firefighters."

Laura tried to figure out what he was talking about so cheerfully. He made it sound like a carnival ride. Then she glanced up at the still-hovering helicopter and the four lines dangling down to the ground and swallowed hard. It wouldn't be dangerous if Johnny was having them do it. Correction, it wouldn't be more dangerous than the alternative. Based on the increasing thickness of the approaching smoke, the alternative was coming quickly.

"I see you each have a small personal pack on your horses. I'd like you to take those and put them on. Please make sure anything important isn't somewhere else, like I see a camera dangling from one of the saddle horns. Do put your camera in your bag; you'll be needing both hands."

Laura helped them get their gear. She also looped each horse's reins through a saddle ring of one of the others. She put Mister Ed at the front of the line, all of the horses trusted him and would probably follow where he led, and Mickey Brown Eyes at the rear was her Mr. Stability anchor. Even now Mickey was the calmest of them all. Some said he was lazy; but Laura knew he was smart enough to not waste energy on getting upset over your average tourist—or major forest fire.

Tim was getting each of the tourists fitted with a harness as Johnny herded them along. He was having them step into the two leg holes, slide the harness up, and then cinch the belt. The two ends of the belt were then snapped into the D-ring at the end of the line dangling from the chopper above.

"Keep both of your hands on the rope the whole time," she could hear Tim whisper to each one, placing the rope in their hands.

"No one afraid of heights, are they?" Johnny made it a casual joke, but continued before anyone could do more than smile at his tone. No time to protest or speak. "What you're going to be doing is called a short-haul. We don't have the ability to lift you each into the helicopter above, but we want to get you out of all this smoke as quickly as possible. So, once you are all in your harnesses and we've checked you for safety, we're going to lift you straight up." He pointed upward.

Laura looked up at the still motionless helicopter, the black paint and red flames looking a little unnerving wreathed in smoke.

"Your airline hostess for the day is named Jeannie Clark and is one of the best helitack pilots ever born. She's going to fly you to the Lodge and set you down pretty as can be in the meadow there. She'll be going slowly, so it will be about a ten-minute flight. Once you're on the ground—not before that please," again that perfect joking tone, "unsnap your harness and step to the side so that she can see you're clear."

Tim had Laura halfway into a harness before she understood what was happening.

"No." she balked back. "No!" She pushed against Tim when he tried to use a gentle force to get her into position.

All of the guests were looking at her wide eyed. The mother and daughter were holding each other's hands rather than the ropes. One of the pairs of newlyweds was hugging as if they'd never see each other again. She was screwing up everything but she couldn't stop herself.

"I can't leave my horses." The guests began relaxing and nodded as if they understood.

Johnny joined Tim's efforts, but she balked hard, just as she imagined Mister Ed would if Johnny tried to harness him up. She knew she was being stupid to ignore the commands of a lead smokejumper, but she couldn't help herself.

Finally he grabbed her arm and dragged her aside.

"Laura! Both ends of the trail are on fire. You're trapped between two heads of fire and they're connected downslope. Right there," he pointed. "In thirty minutes anyone in this canyon is dead."

She nodded her understanding, but she could see Mister Ed. He'd managed, with a toss of his head, to flip his blind off one eye. He was looking right at her.

"Laura!" he shook her.

"I can't!"

———

AKBAR WISHED that he knew how to do that punch they always did in movies, a quick right to the jaw and the person dropped unconscious to the ground; never complaining about a bleeding tongue or loosened teeth afterward. There was no way she'd leave without her horses, unless...

"Laura. You're going. Now. I can't have you as an untrained liability inside the fire. I'll get your horses out. Okay?"

"Really?" Her eyes held hope...and trust. What was it with strong women? She'd cried when he arrived, but now she was clear-eyed. No lip tremble, no whimper. Solid. This was a woman on the verge of giving him all of her trust.

He didn't have a place for that within him. But for the moment he knew what he had to do with it. Let it in and deal with it later.

"Really. Now go!"

She hugged him, whispered in his ear, and rushed to where Tim still held her harness.

Akbar double-checked Tim's work on all of them, perfect as usual. He triple-checked Laura's, then pulled out his radio and called the chopper above.

"Seven ready to go to the Lodge, Jeannie. Nice and easy. They're calm and looking forward to a smooth ride. Laura, ah, has a radio." He'd spotted it on Mister Ed's saddle. Retrieving it, he set the air attack frequency and looped the harness over Laura's head. "Go!"

Jeannie began taking up the slack.

"Everyone hold tight!" he shouted the moment before the first line went taut. With small cries of surprise they were carried aloft.

Laura kept looking down at him between her boots as she drifted upward, dangling and spinning on her own line.

Tim walked up as soon as they were out of sight. "I kinda thought we were supposed to be on that flight as well."

"You care to explain that to him?"

Mister Ed was eyeing them balefully.

Two-Tall shook his head. "Not so much." Then he turned to face downslope. "Well this is going to be fun."

Akbar looked aloft once more but the helicopter was out of sight. Along with it the woman who trusted him so much that she'd whispered, "I love you."

To him.

And he'd thought the burden of trust was going to be the problem.

LAURA CHECKED on the guests dangling with her beneath the helicopter. She had ended up placed by herself on the longest line. The others were hanging above her, face to face in pairs at about ten-foot intervals vertically. At least no one would inadvertently kick someone else in the head. Yet one more piece of the smokies meticulous attention to safety.

"Everyone okay?" she shouted up at them. She had to try a couple of times in order to be heard. Not only were the rotors loud, but their forward progress was making the wind of their passage roar in her ears. They were going at least thirty, maybe faster. She was glad of the sun's afternoon heat on her back and arms. Next time she did this, she'd remind everyone to wear a jacket. A good joke. Despite the beautiful feeling of floating along a hundred feet above the tallest tree in the forest, this was already one time too many.

She received several "Okay!"s and a couple of "Whee!"s as answers.

Then she looked down at the fire. Any sense of amusement or wonder was pounded out of her in a single gasp of breath.

Laura could see why Johnny had told her to stay put: her group had been in the one safe spot. It looked as if the whole side of the mountain was aflame from Little Zigzag right around to Slide Mountain. No, it was that it was all blanketed in smoke.

But Zigzag was certainly ablaze. Both sides of the canyon—to either side of their tiny haven in the firestorm—were spitting fire skyward at the helicopters. Four of the choppers were circling in right now. Even as she watched, one dropped a line of red retardant from a giant orange bucket dangling beneath.

Right behind it, the Firehawk, the biggest of them all, came in very low and released a long flood of red from its belly tank. She could see why the smokies were always so excited when discussing the chopper, it did the work of three or four runs of the smaller chopper.

Looking up at the helicopter Jeannie was flying, she could see that it too had a belly tank and would be returning to the fire the very instant it was rid of her troublesome trail ride.

And it had to get back soon. It was impossible that these tiny gnats could touch the monstrous flames. The choppers were smaller than any single fork of fire lancing skyward. And it seemed the world was full of flames lashing upward above the trees in a mad fury.

She could also see down into the canyon they'd just departed. Laura had left Tim and Johnny and her horses in the heart of the fire. She felt a nauseous swirl of guilt for trapping the men there and insisting they save her animals. She should be the one fighting her own battles. He'd put his and Tim's life on the line for her. No! For her horses. How could she have done such a thing? How could he ever forgive her for doing that to him.

It was almost a slap when they crossed Sand Canyon and began descending toward Timberline Lodge. Between one instant and the next, the canyon was cut off from view, only the plume of smoke marking the desperate battle that was just beginning.

Jeannie lowered them slowly toward the meadow above the Lodge.

Laura remembered her radio and called out her distance to the ground.

Jeannie set her down so soft and easy that it felt as if she were merely taking the next step down a staircase when her boots landed in the tall grass. She moved to assist each couple in getting unraveled and unharnessed as quickly as possible. Some of them were pretty unsteady on their feet, giddy on adrenaline.

The instant she had them all out of their harnesses, she called to Jeannie. "We're clear. Get Johnny and Tim out of there!"

Jeannie was already climbing away when she answered, "Roger that." Someone in the back started pulling up all of the lines.

Laura herded everyone down to the bar. Ordered a free round for everyone and promised them refunds.

"Don't worry about our money," Gus, the newlywed who'd given her the most trouble before, replied. "It was worth it for that ride alone. That was scary amazing!" The others chimed in their agreement.

Didn't they get it? She cried inside. *There were two men out there that she'd placed in a trap with no exits!* She trapped them with a promise and three little words. Had *I love you!* ever been more misused?

"Nonetheless," she kept her tour guide face on for the guests, "we'll give you full refunds or vouchers for other outings. Or lift tickets, whichever you'd prefer. I'm sure that Johnny would be glad to identify a worthy cause to support firefighter families if you wish to turn it into a gift."

"Akbar the Great, you weren't kidding." Gus shook his head. "The guy must be six-foot-six at least."

She didn't bother to correct him. No, Johnny Akbar the Great's size was measured by his heart not his stature.

Laura left the group discussing their grand adventure and headed to the desk to fill in Bess.

"Heard your boyfriend rode to the rescue, sweetie." She tapped the radio behind the desk.

As she counted out the t-shirts all she could do was nod.

He had. Now who was riding to his rescue?

CHAPTER 12

*A**kbar stared up the* slope of Zigzag Canyon, analyzing. The Zigzag River, not much more a rushing stream at this point, tumbled over the boulders lining its bed. The sides of the canyon steepened sharply. He and Tim could get out that way. Maybe. Not with seven horses. They could get lifted out short haul. But not with seven horses.

"Okay, boss. Short of slinging a lot of horses into harnesses, I don't have any brilliant ideas." Tim had moved over to reassure Mister Ed.

Akbar did his best to ignore that the horse that had been rejecting him these last two months was cozying up to Tim like he was his best friend.

The choppers could lift the horses, that wasn't the problem. The problem was rigging a sling quickly and figuring out how to keep the animals from totally freaking out. Frankly, he couldn't believe he'd managed to get the tourists out of there without any panic. It was all Laura's doing. He'd expected to descend into a frantic crowd. Instead, they'd all been quietly standing by their horses' heads to reassure them, despite the forest burning down just out of sight on three sides of them.

Mister Ed pricked his ears downslope.

The fire's roar was building. Hard to estimate time, but one thing was sure, the distance to the blaze was shrinking rapidly.

He got on the radio to Henderson up in his plane. The west was wholly impassable. They were going to let it burn for the moment. The goal was to keep the fire from continuing east around Mount Hood's flank and taking out Timberline Lodge and the two ski areas with all of their equipment, buildings, and condos.

"We lose another half mile and we're going to evacuate that whole side of the mountain. That's all the grassland I have that can burn before we're back into the trees," Henderson was not having a good day. "Where are you?"

"Tim and I are down in the throat of Zigzag Canyon."

"In the— What the hell, Akbar? I'm sending Emily in to get you out of there."

"No, wait." He'd never heard Henderson swear before. Just how ugly was it out there, outside the fire? It certainly wasn't pretty here inside the fire.

"I have a really stupid idea. Need you to give me the *go/no-go* decision. But I will say that if it's *no-go,* I'll let you explain to Laura about three tons of cooked horseflesh."

Then he began laying out his idea. He could feel Henderson cursing, even six thousand feet above them with his microphone turned off.

LAURA COULDN'T STAND it one moment longer. Everyone had their twenty dollar t-shirts and the mood was high. Already their adventure was being shared with other guests, in the past tense.

She headed out through the same "Employee's Door" she'd used to avoid Grayson Clyde Masterson, their calls to come join them still ringing in her ears. This time, once she was out the back door, she didn't circle around to the parking lot to make good her escape.

Without thinking about it, she started out striding up the meadow behind the Lodge, past where the helicopter had dropped them. She was at a fast trot by they time she passed the base of the Magic Mile lift that could whisk her up to the ice and snow which still covered the upper slopes deeply. After five hundred feet of elevation gain at a run, she picked up the PCT. When her feet hit the trail, she was moving flat out. It was a roughshod run in her riding boots, but she covered the ground fast.

In just two miles she came up behind the line of smokies and slowed her pace. Her trail group had been so close to making it back before they were cut off.

What had been a smoke-clogged canyon thirty minutes earlier, was now a towering cloud reaching far past the mountain's peak. The wind currents that whipped the peak year round were ripping the top off the smoke plume and dragging it over the peak. It was hard to tell if the glacier was blackened by the shadow of the looming cloud or if a coating of ash now covered the usually blinding white snow.

The trail itself led through the smokies' position and into a wall of tangled smoke and flame, both so thick it was impossible to discern one from the other in the swirling mass.

From here, it looked like the smokies were standing right up against the flame. But as she drew closer, she could see that the distances were deceptive and a roll of the landscape made the flames appear closer than they actually were.

Still, her feet stumbled to a halt well back of the smokie's line. Smoke loomed above her. That wasn't surprising except in its massive thickness. But she also saw black clouds billowing overhead when she looked up. Way up. It towered dozens of stories above them, and Johnny's crew was moving along at the same relaxed pace they'd used while cleaning up her trees. Not relaxed, sustainable for hour after hour.

It was an impossible world, but they worked in it. One of them spotted her and left the line to come over and talk to her.

"Hi Laura." It was Krista, the powerful Nordic woman. "You weren't planning on coming any closer, were you?" She pulled out a water bottle and offered it to Laura first before taking a drink herself.

"Nearer the flame?" she shook her head. "No. Not even another step."

"Good. Makes you a smart woman. It's going pretty well so far."

Laura looked at the conflagration before her. "This is well?"

"So far. Still a little early to tell. But I think we'll be able to hold this side of the fire. Ox and Chas have already had to retreat twice. The northwest side is quite ugly at the moment for such a little fire. Glad you called it in as early as you did."

Laura didn't feel so bad any more about flying out of the fire zone. If this wasn't ugly, she couldn't imagine something like the Tillamook Burn that Johnny had fought before they met.

"Are they...?" She couldn't form the question.

"Out? No. Not yet."

Laura sagged. She'd actually been trying to ask if she'd killed them. *Not yet* was the answer there as well.

"But stay right here. You'll see some serious shit here real soon." Krista, apparently done with her break, stuffed away her water bottle and picked up the axe she'd rested on the ground while they talked. "Of course if it doesn't work, they'll be going into the shelters, and that would be very bad."

The shelters. Small foil tents that firefighters hid beneath if they were caught in the middle of an inescapable fire. That was a tool of absolute last resort. This had been her doing. She'd put their lives at risk by insisting he save her horses. No. Johnny wouldn't take risks unnecessarily. Krista was being pessimistic, or maybe preparing her in case things went badly.

"But we think we've got it," Krista reassured her. "The ICA approved Akbar's plan."

Johnny had a plan. His plans were always good, weren't they? She wavered on the edge of being sick as the world spun. Please let his plan work. Let him come back to her and not hate her for what she'd done to him.

"Arson is such a bitch." Krista headed away.

It took Laura a moment to process that and she had to sprint up to

Krista. Laura grabbed her arm and spun her back before she reached her crew. "Arson?"

Krista nodded, "Fire Marshall still needs to investigate, but after a while you know it when you see it. Somebody wanted to burn up this canyon for some reason. Gotta go."

For the life of her, Laura couldn't imagine why someone would do that.

"SLIT THE T-SHIRTS LIKE THIS," Akbar demonstrated. He pulled out his big knife and untucked the shirt from Mickey's bridle. He slit it vertically from mid-chest down to a few inches above the hem, right through both the front and the back. Then he returned to the horse and Mickey shied away.

He tucked his knife away, cooed at the horse, and tried again with little better luck. If Mister Ed had turned the whole troop against him, this was going to get difficult.

"Try facing him upslope," Tim suggested as he sliced Mister Ed's t-shirt to match the one Akbar had cut.

Once facing upslope, away from the fire, Mickey became more manageable. Akbar tucked the sides and top of t-shirt back into place, dragging the vertical slit wide open in front of the horse's face. Mickey could see forward through the gap in the material, but it acted like a blinder to either side.

He and Tim worked down the line until all seven horses were unmasked, but wore their t-shirt blinders.

"Okay," Akbar went up to Mister Ed. "This is about to get ugly, horse. But you and I are going to have to put aside for the moment that there's a woman out there who loves both of us, and we gotta cooperate if we're going to make this work."

"She loves you?" Tim practically shouted at him.

"That's what she said anyway."

"And you aren't runnin' for the high hills?"

"Hello," Akbar waved a hand. "Fire on every side. Nowhere to run."

"She actually said it out loud?"

"Yeah, more of a whisper actually. This ear," he tapped it and then felt really stupid. "About ten seconds before we launched her into the sky."

"Shit! And I thought we were just being nice and saving some horses. Love! Awesome!" Tim's slap on his back made a thunderclap sound against his Nomex gear, startling the horses.

"Well done, Two-Tall."

"She loves *you*. You sure she's right in the head?" Tim was shaking his head and speaking mostly to himself. "Don't that beat all. She got any crazy sisters?"

"Only child."

"Shit!"

"You about ready to ride? They should be ready for us in about five minutes." Akbar needed a subject change badly, but they weren't going anywhere just yet. Imagining Tim in love was a little too strange. Almost as bad as, well...yeah...almost as bad as imagining himself in love.

"Small problem with your plan, Great One."

"What's that?"

Tim actually looked a little helpless. "I've never ridden a horse."

Akbar rolled his eyes and led him back to Mickey. If there was ever a horse that would make sure his rider stayed aboard it was Mickey. They lengthened the stirrups down to the last notch, it was a close thing, but it would be good enough for Tim to ride without looking too much like an oversized jockey perched atop the horse.

Of course, he'd planned to bring up the rear on Mickey. This meant that...crap! He was going to be riding Mister Ed.

He moved back to the head of the line to negotiate a truce with a horse that hated him.

———————

LAURA HAD a front row seat and wished she'd stayed at the Lodge and had a drink with the guests. Several. Gotten good and stinking drunk.

Instead, she was stone cold sober, sitting and waiting. Krista had finally banished her to this boulder because she kept trying to approach the blaze in hopes of the impossible, spotting Johnny and Tim.

Not a hundred yards ahead of her, the Pacific Crest Trail disappeared into flame. Between her and the flames, the trees and grasses were dark red with heavy layers of retardant chemicals dropped by the helicopters. It should keep any flames from escaping in her direction.

She knew from experience that fifty yards into the flame, the level terrain took a sharp dip down into the narrow heart of the canyon.

Right now, the smokies were beginning an attack on the fire. They were on the far side of the fire, just downslope of the Pacific Crest Trail and this time they were getting close to the flames. Hadn't Johnny told her it meant things were going wrong when that happened? She shoved that thought aside hard.

The smokies were felling trees away from the trail to either side as if driving a wedge sideways into the fire right down the trail. A hose team was coming up close behind.

One of the choppers came in low overhead and dropped a load of water, some of it splashing on the smokies they were so close to the fire. Instead of dousing the leading edge of the fire, which was further upslope, they were making a beeline into the flank of the conflagration. Another chopper followed, then another and another until all five had passed overhead and unloaded in rapid succession right in line with the trail.

Water. They weren't dumping retardant to stop the spread of fire, they were dumping water to fight it directly.

The smokies followed the water-soaked trail right into the fire. They felled trees that still had burning branches here and there, and kept driving forward.

Less than five minutes later the line of choppers was back. Once again, the four smaller ones made successive water drops straight into the fire. Then the Firehawk roared in and dumped a massive load of the red retardant.

Some of it splattered on the ground crew, but most of it protected the drenched stretch of trail.

She could see what they were doing. It was crazy. Johnny had told her that you flanked and headed off a fire. That you never went straight at the flames. Yet here they were cutting a path directly into the inferno. It was Akbar the Great kind of crazy. It had to be him who thought this up.

Laura looked at their progress. If she were leading the crew, she wouldn't dare take them much farther into the woods. This had to be it.

She wanted to hold her breath, but her heart was pounding so hard she could barely get enough air at this altitude. They were right at six thousand feet. Although she spent her days at this altitude, she slept thousands of feet lower.

This time when the helicopters made their run, the smokies didn't drive further in. Instead they retreated back to their starting position not a hundred yards from her.

One by one the helicopters roared by, a bare hundred feet over her head, shot over the edge of the canyon and actually disappeared downward out of sight as they did their drops.

Now she did hold her breath until each chopper popped back into view at the far end of its run, deep inside the smoke, but turning aside before entering the massive main plume.

Just as she was doing, the smokies were craning their necks to watch down the newly visible portion of the Pacific Crest Trail.

Softly at first. Growing rapidly. A sound she knew as well as her own heartbeat. The earth pounding boom of seven horses moving up the hard trail at a full gallop.

Riding smoothly atop Mister Ed rode Akbar the Great.

And, hanging on for dear life in Mickey's saddle, Two-Tall Tim brought up the rear.

CHAPTER 13

here wasn't time for Laura to even speak to Johnny at the fire. He managed to stop the whole train of horses not a dozen paces from her perch. He leapt to the ground as she slithered down from her boulder.

He kissed her, grinned, and slapped her butt, before turning and sprinting back toward the fire. He was on the radio before he was even fully turned away. Many men had slapped her butt. And almost every one had carried the bright red mark on their cheek of the hardest slap she could deliver.

Johnny's slap told her that life was so damn good that she could barely keep the feeling inside. She wanted to dance as she hugged Mister Ed's nose. He was blowing hard with the intensity of the brief run through the close flames, but his ears were pricked forward and his tail whipped about with his pleasure at being out of the fire and with her again.

Two-Tall clambered down, offered her a sickly smile, then chased his friend's heels back to fight the fire.

The horses were positively giddy as she led them back down the trail to the Lodge. In their corral she carefully tended each one, giving them all extra oats. Word soon filtered up to the Lodge that the horses were back. Her entire ride group came down to the corral, much the worse for their time in the bar. Others joined in to see the horses who had galloped through the flames. Bess must be spreading the word far and wide.

Laura only told the story once. The tour group was much more somber when she finished her tale of what two men had done to save seven horses. She then left it to the voluble Gus and his fiancée to retell and embellish the tale.

After that, she kept quiet, calmed her horses and herself.

And did her best not to smile too much at the image of her white knight, in char-dusted yellow Nomex and a hardhat, riding hell bent for leather out of the flames.

IT WAS DAWN by the time Akbar came off the line. He'd turned down the chopper ride and followed the trail east toward the Lodge. He was dog tired, but they'd beaten down the southeastern branch of the fire.

The deep slice that Krista's team and the choppers had cut into the fire to clear his escape route along the trail had been held. And it was rapidly tied into the flanking retardant they'd been building along the edge of the canyon. The fight to contain it had been close, but they'd held it at bay while the choppers trapped the upper lines of the fire from spreading sideways.

They'd let the flames above the trail run up the mountain to die above the timberline, on the barren rocks left behind by the summer's retreating snow. The edge of the fire defined by the southern ridge of Zigzag Canyon and the right angle slice of the PCT had been held. There was no need to evacuate the Lodge or the ski areas.

The north side was still in play, but a Hotshot team had become available and one of the new high-capacity fixed-wing air tankers would be on site as soon as the sun was up. The BAe-146 with its four jet engines could deliver three times the load of the Firehawk. So, he'd left half of his smoke team embedded with the Hotshots, and released the other half when a mop-up crew had arrived at his and Krista's side of the fire.

It felt good to simply walk off the high tension and adrenalin of the firefight, but he was thankful for the level trail. A day and a night on the front lines had left him a little lightheaded. The morning chill sliding downslope from the ice fields slowly cooled his skin until he was glad of the exercise to keep him warm. He should have kept his jacket when he was tossing his gear aboard the chopper headed back to camp.

He wanted to check on the horses, see if Mister Ed was willing to talk to him, and he'd bet Laura would be up on the mountain early this morning.

Akbar reached the corral below the Lodge as the sun edged over the mountain peaks to the east and splashed long dark shadows that distorted the world.

The horses were still asleep. He leaned on the corral rail and watched them for a while.

Laura had trusted him and he'd found a way to deliver. Women who trusted Akbar were usually in for a rude shock somewhere along the way. But for Laura, he'd been driven to a creative solution by his desire to deserve her trust. That the tactic had ultimately led to the containment of the fire had entered into his plan, but he hadn't actually expected it to work as well as it had.

He liked the way it felt that she'd trusted him. And that he'd proven himself trustworthy. He also knew there'd have been no blame if he hadn't saved the horses; it wasn't something a woman like her would do. There'd be hurt and pain and tears and all of those other things he'd always done his best to avoid, but there would never be blame. Like his crew, she simply knew he'd always do his best.

Akbar realized that the big gelding was watching him from across the corral.

"Yeah, who are we kidding?" he whispered softer than the dawn. "Trust isn't the question that's bothering us, is it?"

Mister Ed shook his head, flipping his dark brown mane back and forth and making his big ears flop ridiculously.

"It's that she loves us."

The horse offered a snort.

At the sound, Akbar spotted movement over in the corner of the corral. On a bed made of straw bales and a couple of horse blankets, Laura shifted position slightly, then slid back into sleep.

As quietly as he could, he clambered over the fence. He stopped a step away and looked down at her. Love was a word that he'd heard a lot in his family; it was a family sort of word.

How hard would it be to imagine Laura in a family sort of way? Not very hard at all once he tried it. Akbar found it easy to picture living in the beautiful cabin in the woods, a small herd of horses dancing about the corral, maybe even a kid. Nope, not hard to picture at all.

If he put her *I love you* in a place down inside himself, it made perfect sense.

He heard the slow clip-clop of the big tan gelding coming up behind him across the hard-packed earth. Mister Ed stopped with his head beside Akbar's shoulder. He rubbed the horse's nose as they looked down at the sleeping woman together.

"Yes," he told the horse. "She makes it real easy to imagine."

"Hey, lover," Laura greeted him with a sleepy voice, looking up at him with those half-lidded honey-gold eyes.

"Hey, my love," he had to try it out. Oddly enough, it wasn't scary at all. It fit inside him as if he'd been waiting his whole life for that one missing piece.

She lifted one edge of the blanket. He left the horse and slid against her warmth, holding her long into the brightening day.

CHAPTER 14

*I*t *was precisely one* week later when Akbar was jerked awake—shortly before dawn—by the massive thunderclap of a huge explosion. Laura's bedroom was briefly lit by a light as bright as a lightning bolt. No lightning had been predicted, anywhere in the state.

He'd heard a sound like it once near the end of the New Tillamook Burn. A massive explosion had flattened a large circle of trees at the northern end of the fire. No one was talking about it; "abandoned propane tank" the newspapers had reported. Yeah, sure. A propane tank sitting out in the middle of the Tillamook State Forest. He hadn't been able to figure out what it was. He could tell Jeannie knew, but she'd looked grim and gone tight-lipped when he'd asked.

This blast was close, loud. Moments later, a second one lit the pre-dawn sky again and rattled the windows an instant later. It was close. No time to count the seconds to estimate the strike's distance.

He was out on the porch with Laura close beside him. Only a hand in front of her kept her from running naked into the woods to see what happened. He waited for it, saw the underlit smoke climbing into the cloudless, pre-dawn sky above the tall trees.

There was a fire burning below the black smoke. A second tower of smoke rolled skyward to the south of the first one.

By instinct he'd grabbed his radio from the charger as they'd run out onto the porch.

"Grab our boots!" They'd left them on the porch last night. "Come on!" He wasn't letting go of her hand or his radio until he had them out in the open. As soon as she had the boots, he sprinted over to his truck and called out on the radio.

"MHA base. Someone there? Wake up!" he shouted into the mike. Mark or TJ or someone was bound to have the radio near their bed turned on.

"MHA base," Jeannie's voice was blurred with sleep. Mark's acknowledgement followed a moment later.

"I have a double-explosion at Laura's cabin. Big ones. We have fire in the woods." He didn't need to give any more details.

"Roger, we're coming!" Mark's answer was wide awake and there was a heterodyne squeal as Jeannie's response overlapped his. He could hear the siren already climbing in the background of the dual radio call.

He tossed the radio on the hood of his truck and dug into his ready box. Laura had been too reluctant about leaving his side in the Zigzag Canyon fire, no way would he be able to get her somewhere safe if her cabin was threatened. He glanced up at the two smoke columns against the pinking sky. The tips of the smoke cloud were arrowing right toward them. Not much breeze, but what there was of it would drive the fire right at them.

"Here," he dug out the long cotton underwear and a tossed a spare set at Laura. "We've got to get some clothes on."

Without a word, she dragged them on. In moments they were both outfitted in Nomex, hardhats, and were lacing up their boots. His beautiful lady was a calm center, his stable rock. How he had lived all these years without her, he couldn't imagine. It was completely an extra added bonus that she looked so goddamn cute in a hardhat.

He grabbed both of her shoulders and turned her to face him. Her eyes were wide and her breathing rapid—nowhere near panic but not as focused as he'd like.

Akbar pulled her in briefly and kissed her. When he checked again, she swallowed hard, nodded once, and he could see the panic recede a few more steps. Getting to grab her butt was just one of the perks of being in love with her.

"Okay. First thing you do is go to the cabin, get your radio and set it on my frequency. After that, get your hose running and start soaking the side of the cabin toward the fire. You went with a metal roof, so don't worry about that much. Get the logs of the cabin walls and the first ten feet of ground as wet as you can. And Laura?"

He waited until he got the verbal, "Yes?" meaning she was present and listening.

"If I tell you to run, you don't ask, you don't hesitate, you goddamn run. Roger that?"

She opened her mouth to protest and he cut her off.

"I am so not going to lose the woman I plan to spend the rest of my life with to some goddamn arsonist over a cabin we can always rebuild together. Are we clear now?"

Laura nodded, hesitantly at first, then more emphatically as the message sank in. Then she hit him with one of her glowing smiles and he felt taller than Tim.

He turned her, aimed her at the cabin, and slapped her butt to get her moving. He took the precious few seconds to watch her find her feet and break into a sprint. Not quite how he'd ever pictured proposing to a woman, but then Laura wasn't quite like any woman he'd ever met, so it fit.

Then he grabbed an axe, but left the chainsaw. This fire was too close to fight with a firebreak, they were going to have to fight it on the ground. He stuffed his radio into its pouch on the front of his jacket at his left shoulder. A quick double-click came out the speaker of someone keying their own radio. He looked over to see Laura emerging from the cabin holding up her own handheld.

Akbar turned and headed into the woods. His buddies were still ten minutes out, so it was too dangerous to approach the fire directly.

Instead, he circled wide of the flames avoiding the road and began trotting in a wide circle through the woods toward the fire's origin.

LAURA HAD both of her hoses running and was glad that she'd put down the money for the higher-powered well pump. She'd merely thought to save time when filling the horses' watering trough. Now she held the two nozzles side by side and swept them up and down the side of the log cabin and soaked the perimeter ground—both grass and planting beds.

A glance over her shoulder showed the two columns of smoke merging into one larger one. In the growing light she could see that they weren't as black as she'd first thought. But they had been. As black as...

Arsonist. The word finally snuck back into her memory. As black as a gasoline fire. By the size of the explosions, a lot of gasoline. And the smoke was changing color as it began burning the forest.

Had whoever lit the fire even known her cabin was here? It was well hidden.

Arsonist. It was a hell of an odd word to have in a marriage proposal. She felt absolutely ridiculous to be standing here in full fire-fighter's gear, spraying her home to protect it from a lunatic's fire. That she was also grinning like an idiot really put her sanity in question.

The woman I plan to spend the rest of my life with. That so worked for her. She was head over heels gone on her charging knight in Nomex yellow. She hoped that he understood her smile was the loudest *yes* that she'd been able to give at the moment. His proposal had simply filled her too much for any words.

The smoke had spread wide across the morning sky by the time she'd sprayed down the closest side of the log cabin and yard. She started back down the length to soak it more thoroughly when she heard the little lawnmower sound of the drone, followed shortly by the thudding beat of a helicopter arriving overhead.

She'd come to appreciate that sound deeply.

Now they could help Johnny fight the fire. She looked all around the clearing, but could see no sign of him. She considered radioing him to see where he was, but didn't want to interrupt him wherever he had gotten to.

AKBAR DIALED down the volume on his radio as he moved from tree to tree through the forest. The fire was still so newly started that there wasn't a "black" yet where the fire had burned and left behind nothing but char. He skirted the trailing edge of the fire seeking the origin, letting the fire's roar mask any sounds he made. It wasn't the full-throated freight train of a monster fire yet, but it was definitely up to accelerating semi-truck. A whole line of them.

Please. Please. Please, let the arsonist still be here admiring his handi-work. According to his training, that was not the least unusual. They craved the fire and wanted to watch it burn. He didn't know what he'd do when he found the guy, but the Pulaski fire axe felt good and solid in Akbar's hand.

Whatever accelerant the bastard had used to start the blaze had been a powerful one. Gasoline fit the profile.

He stopped beside a couple of white-barked aspens.

The Fire Marshall's report had identified gasoline as the accelerant at the four-point origin of the Zigzag fire.

If it was the same arsonist, what else did the two fires have in common?

Shit! He'd been so stupid.

He turned and sprinted back toward the cabin hugging the encircling fire as closely as he dared to find the shortest route back.

The only other common factor between the two fires was Laura.

LAURA HAD KEPT GLANCING over her shoulder as she worked the hoses.

She'd now sprayed both the front and back of her home as well as repeating her coverage on the side toward the flames. She had planted alternating rhododendrons and red-twig dogwoods along this side of the cabin, one so pretty in the spring, the other in the winter. She began working on the shrubs.

A man came out of the woods as another helicopter joined the first one above the fire. Too tall for Johnny, too short for Tim, and too narrow-shouldered for Ox. She shifted the hoses further along the cabin wall.

When she looked back, the man was much closer. His clothing was wrong. He'd lost his hardhat somewhere. He had dark hair and patrician features.

It only took her a moment to attach a name to the face, Grayson Clyde Masterson.

"Hello Laura."

Her world slowed down in that instant. Slowed down so much that she couldn't help but assume it was some sort of a human survival mechanism. She even had time to be surprised at the feeling of her heightened perception.

The fires suddenly made sense. Grayson had burned a whole side of Mount Hood, but he'd done it very carefully. Everything had been perfectly timed to trap her party in the heart of Zigzag Canyon. Only Johnny's quick work had saved the day and the mountain.

Grayson had lit these fires as well. She had refused him passage to her bed and instead taken in another who would appear inferior to Grayson in every single way: stature, heritage, and career.

Laura also had time to note what Grayson was carrying. In one hand, a wine bottle with a rag dangling out of the top. In the other, a small bit of silver that might be a lighter.

Behind him, descending so fast it looked as if it was about to crash, a helicopter plummeted toward her horse corral. It pulled up at the last second. Someone who'd been in the cargo bay dove out the door, doing a rolling landing, and began sprinting in her direction.

Still in her slow motion world, she saw Grayson flick his lighter and move it toward the wick on his Molotov cocktail.

It was Mark leaping over the corral fence, too far away to help.

Around the side of the house, Johnny appeared. One moment not there, the next running at Grayson.

He too would be too late.

She saw the instant that Grayson noticed Johnny's approach. His sneer twisted into a snarl. The moment before, he'd probably been planning to burn her cabin right before her eyes. Now he planned to burn her lover.

The cold of the twinned brass hose nozzles still chilled her hand.

Grayson lit his incendiary at the same moment she raised the hoses from where they'd been drowning a rhododendron. He cocked his arm back to heave the flaming bottle at the oncoming Johnny.

She hit the bottle with both nozzles. It was knocked out of Grayson's hands and fell to the ground behind Grayson, not a dozen paces from her or her cabin. But it didn't break. Instead it merely rolled in slow motion, still aflame as she continued shifting the hose toward her next target.

The twin sprays of water caught Grayson full in the face at the same moment that Johnny slammed his axe handle into Grayson's gut.

Grayson stumbled back.

It took forever for him to fall. Like a tree falling, first only a look of surprise to indicate the loss of balance. Then flailing arms. Then—

Laura couldn't look away from the unfolding disaster.

AKBAR DOVE AT LAURA, driving her to the ground with a flying full-body tackle as the gas-filled wine bottle exploded, splashing a circle of fire for a dozen feet in every direction.

Some of it struck the cabin wall.

It had also coated the back of her gear in flame. He kept her in a bear hug and rolled her away from the flame, over and over on the muddy ground until she was extinguished.

Once he was sure the flames on her were fully out, he held her at arms' length and checked her. She blinked dazedly, but appeared fine. She might not even have known she'd been on fire.

He glanced over his shoulder to make sure he wasn't burning as well. Smoulders from his own gear indicated that he had been, but he appeared to be unscathed as well.

Then he saw the man in black jeans and turtleneck. He lay unconscious in the center of the fire. Akbar's first reaction was to figure out how to get him out, but it was way too hot, he couldn't get close enough.

Laura started to turn around and he wrapped his arms around her to keep her facing the log wall.

Mark too stood a dozen yards back from the flame. He had his radio out and moments later they were all awash in a thousand gallons of water that hammered down out of the sky.

The deluge tumbled Akbar and Laura into the side of the cabin. Again, he managed to protect her and take most of the hit himself. Mark was knocked flat on his back into the mud.

But Emily had dead-centered the fire. It was completely out. However, one glance was enough to show that there was no help for the man who'd lain in the center of the flames. He lay face down in the pool of water, motionless, most of his skin already blackened.

Akbar managed to get Laura up and around the corner of the building without her seeing anything. There were some memories she didn't need to have. He sat her down in the porch chair by the front door and knelt in front of her.

"Hey, Space Ace."

Her reply was slow, but lucid, "Hey yourself, Fire Boy." Then she startled and tried to rise.

Akbar kept her trapped in the chair on the front porch.

"My cabin?" She pushed at him.

"Hardly even any scorch marks. You did a great job of soaking it down. Though I'll need to replace the living room window." Either the blast of the fire or the impact of the helicopter's water drop had blown the glass inward. But that was the only damage he'd noticed.

She settled back into the chair. "I'm guessing Grayson is dead by his own flame and that's why you shuffled me over here so fast."

Grayson? There hadn't been time to recognize him, only to attack. Damn it! Akbar should have cut the bloody rope on the guy back when he had the chance up on the glacier. Of course if he had, he'd have been in jail for life. But Grayson hadn't targeted him. Somewhere in his demented reasoning, he'd targeted Laura for refusing him. Well, no regrets here.

"I can see the fire," Laura was looking over his shoulder. Her voice was still a little disconnected.

He turned to check the woods. Through the trees that they'd dead-limbed, they had a clear view of the forest beyond. The flames had burned their way toward the cabin, but stalled at the line where his crew had done the clean-up. Not enough heat to torch the trees, and not enough dry fuel to continue forward.

High in the morning sky, he could see the helicopters circling above, dropping loads of water down on the leading edge of the fire. Against the backdrop of the flames, he could see his smoke team moving steadily along the forest floor, keeping the flame's boundary contained. This fire would be out in hours. He'd see to the mop-up himself to make sure there were no hidden hotspots that could reignite, but for now, they didn't need him.

Mark looked around the corner of the cabin and gave him a thumbs up. The remains of one idiot arsonist were cleaned up and gone. He'd already been beholden to Mark, but now he owed him big time. At least a brew down at the Doghouse.

"They've contained the fire," he reassured Laura. "The fire won't get near you, or your home."

She looked back at him. Her expression was no longer dazed. She was studying him intently from beneath the brim of her yellow hardhat.

He brushed a hand over her muddy cheek. Looked again at her char- and mud-stained Nomex to make sure she was uninjured. She was fine. She was so very fine.

"You said some things earlier, Fire Boy."

He had.

She raised her eyebrows at him rather than speaking, but allowed her smile out to play a bit.

He'd talked about a lifetime together. Behind that simple statement was marriage, kids, and years upon years lit through and through with trust and love.

Akbar was already kneeling at her booted feet. He couldn't ask for more than this woman was offering. Not ever. It was the best offer of his entire life.

He looked up into those honey-gold eyes alight with the new day and answered with all of his heart.

"Those things I said, Space Ace? I meant every single word."

TO KEEP BURNING UP THE PAGES IN THIS SERIES, READ:

(EXCERPT)

WILDFIRE AT LARCH CREEK
(EXCERPT)

wo-Tall Tim Harada leaned over Akbar the Great's shoulder to look out the rear door of the DC-3 airplane.

"Ugly," he shouted over the roar of the engine and wind.

Akbar nodded rather than trying to speak.

Since ugly was their day job, it didn't bother Tim much, but this was worse than usual. It would be their fourth smokejump in nine days on the same fire. The Cottonwood Peak Fire was being a total pain in the butt, even worse than usual for a wildfire. Every time they blocked it in one direction, the swirling winds would turnabout and drive the fire toward a new point on the compass. Typical for the Siskiyou Mountains of northern California, but still a pain.

Akbar tossed out a pair of crepe paper streamers and they watched together. The foot-wide streamers caught wind and curled, loop-the-looped through vortices, and reversed direction at least three times. Pretty much the worst conditions possible for a parachute jump.

"It's what we live for!"

Akbar nodded and Tim didn't have to see his best friend's face to know about the fierce wildness of his white grin on his Indian-dark face. Or the matching one against his own part-Vietnamese coloring. Many women told him that his mixed Viet, French-Canadian, and

Oklahoman blood made him intriguingly exotic—a fact that had never hurt his prospects in the bar.

The two of them were the first-stick smokejumpers for Mount Hood Aviation, the best freelance firefighters of them all. This was—however moronic—*precisely* what they lived for. He'd followed Akbar the Great's lead for five years and the two of them had climbed right to the top.

"Race you," Akbar shouted then got on the radio and called directions about the best line of attack to "DC"—who earned his nickname from his initials matching the DC-3 jump plane he piloted.

Tim moved to give the deployment plan to the other five sticks still waiting on their seats; no need to double check it with Akbar, the best approach was obvious. Heck, this was the top crew. The other smokies barely needed the briefing; they'd all been watching through their windows as the streamers cavorted in the chaotic winds.

Then, while DC turned to pass back over the jump zone, he and Akbar checked each others' gear. Hard hat with heavy mesh face shield, Nomex fire suit tight at the throat, cinched at the waist, and tucked in the boots. Parachute and reserve properly buckled, with the static line clipped to the wire above the DC-3's jump door. Pulaski fire axe, fire shelter, personal gear bag, chain saw on a long rope tether, gas can...the list went on, and through long practice took them under ten seconds to verify.

Five years they'd been jumping together, the last two as lead stick. Tim's body ached, his head swam with fatigue, and he was already hungry though they'd just eaten a full meal at base camp and a couple energy bars on the short flight back to the fire. All the symptoms were typical for a long fire.

DC called them on close approach. Once more Akbar leaned out the door, staying low enough for Tim to lean out over him. Not too tough as Akbar was a total shrimp and Tim had earned the "Two-Tall" nickname for being two Akbars tall. He wasn't called Akbar the Great for his height, but rather for his powerful build and unstoppable energy on the fire line.

"Let's get it done and..." Tim shouted in Akbar's ear as they approached the jump point.

"...come home to Mama!" and Akbar was gone.

Tim actually hesitated before launching himself after Akbar and ended up a hundred yards behind him.

Come home to Mama? Akbar had always finished the line, *Go get the girls.* Ever since the wedding, Akbar had gotten all weird in the head. Just because he was married and happy was no excuse to—

The static line yanked his chute. He dropped below the tail of the DC-3—always felt as if he had to duck, but doorways on the ground did the same thing to him—and the chute caught air and jerked him hard in the groin.

The smoke washed across the sky. High, thin cirrus clouds promised an incoming weather change, but wasn't going to help them much today. The sun was still pounding the wilderness below with a scorching, desiccating heat that turned trees into firebrands at a single spark.

The Cottonwood Peak Fire was chewing across some hellacious terrain. Hillsides so steep that some places you needed mountaineering gear to go chase the flames. Hundred-and-fifty foot Doug firs popping off like fireworks. Ninety-six thousand acres, seventy percent contained and a fire as angry as could be that they were beating it down.

Tim yanked on the parachute's control lines as the winds caught him and tried to fling him back upward into the sky. On a jump like this you spent as much time making sure that the chute didn't tangle with itself in the chaotic winds as you did trying to land somewhere reasonable.

Akbar had called it right though. They had to hit high on this ridge and hold it. If not, that uncontained thirty percent of the wildfire was going to light up a whole new valley to the east and the residents of Hornbrook, California were going to have a really bad day.

His chute spun him around to face west toward the heart of the blaze. Whoever had rated this as seventy percent contained clearly needed his head examined. Whole hillsides were still alight with flame. It was only because the MHA smokies had cut so many fire-breaks over the last eight days, combined with the constant pounding of the big Firehawk helicopters dumping retardant loads every which way, that the whole mountain range wasn't on fire.

Tim spotted Akbar. Below and to the north. Damn but that guy could fly a chute. Tim dove hard after him.

Come home to Mama! Yeesh! But the dog had also found the perfect lady. Laura Jenson: wilderness guide, expert horsewoman—who was still trying to get Tim up on one of her beasts—and who was really good for Akbar. But it was as if Tim no longer recognized his best friend.

They used to crawl out of a fire, sack out in the bunks for sixteen-straight, then go hit the bars. *What do I do for a living? I parachute out of airplanes to fight wildfires by hand.* It wowed the women every time, gained them pick of the crop.

Now when Akbar hit the ground, Laura would be waiting in her truck and they'd disappear to her little cabin in the woods. What was up with that anyway?

available at fine retailers everywhere

TELL THE WORLD THIS BOOK WAS		
GOOD *very*	BAD	SO-SO

ABOUT THE AUTHOR

M.L. Buchman started the first of, what is now over 50 novels and even more short stories, while flying from South Korea to ride his bicycle across the Australian Outback. All part of a solo around-the-world bicycle trip (a mid-life crisis on wheels) that ultimately launched his writing career.

Booklist has selected his military and firefighter series(es) as 3-time "Top 10 Romance of the Year." NPR and Barnes & Noble have named other titles "Best 5 Romance of the Year." In 2016 he was a finalist for RWA's prestigious RITA award.

He has flown and jumped out of airplanes, can single-hand a fifty-foot sailboat, and has designed and built two houses. In between writing, he also quilts. M. L. is constantly amazed at what you can do with a degree in Geophysics. He also writes: contemporary romance, thrillers, and fantasy.

More info and a free novel for subscribing to his newsletter at: www.mlbuchman.com

Join the conversation:
www.mlbuchman.com

Other works by M. L. Buchman:

SIGN UP FOR M. L. BUCHMAN'S NEWSLETTER TODAY

and receive:
Release News
Free Short Stories
a Free novel

Do it today. Do it now.
www.mlbuchman.com/newsletter

CPSIA information can be obtained
at www.ICGtesting.com
Printed in the USA
FSHW021908081019
62814FS